Team Spirit

Samantha Alexander lives in Lincolnshire with a variety of animals including her thoroughbred horse, Bunny, and a pet goose called Bertie. Her schedule is almost as busy and exciting as her plots – she writes a number of columns for newspapers and magazines, is a teenage agony aunt for BBC Radio Leeds and in her spare time she regularly competes in dressage and showjumping.

Also by Samantha Alexander
and available from Macmillan

RIDERS

1 Will to Win
3 Peak Performance   January 1997
4 Rising Star   February 1997

HOLLYWELL STABLES

1 Flying Start
2 The Gamble
3 Revenge
4 Fame
5 The Mission
6 Trapped
7 Running Wild
8 Secrets

RIDERS

2

Team Spirit

SAMANTHA ALEXANDER

MACMILLAN CHILDREN'S BOOKS

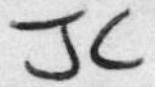

First published 1996 by
Macmillan Children's Books
a division of Macmillan Publishers Ltd
25 Eccleston Place, London SW1W 9NF
and Basingstoke

Associated companies throughout the world

ISBN 0 330 34534 6

1 3 5 7 9 8 6 4 2

A CIP catalogue record for this book is available from the British Library.

Typeset by Intype London Ltd
Printed by Mackays of Chatham PLC, Chatham, Kent.

To Daisy, my basset hound, whose antics feature so strongly throughout this series. The best dog ever.

Samantha Alexander and Macmillan Children's Books would like to thank *Horse and Pony* magazine for helping us by running a competition to find our cover girl, Sally Johnson. Look out for more about the **Riders** and **Hollywell Stables** series in *Horse and Pony* magazine and find out more about Samantha by reading her agony column in every issue.

Macmillan Children's Books would also like to thank Chris White; and David Burrows and all at Sandridgebury Stables, especially Toby and his owner Sylvie.

And finally thanks to Angela Clarke from Ride-Away in Sutton-on-Forest, Yorkshire for providing the riding clothes, hats and boots featured on the covers.

CHARACTERS

Alexandra Johnson Our heroine. 14 years old. Blonde, brown eyes. Ambitious, strong-willed and determined to become a top eventer. Owns Barney, a 14.2 hh dun with black points.

Ash Burgess Our hero. 19 years old. Blond hair, blue eyes, flashy smile. Very promising young eventer. He runs the livery stables for his parents. His star horse is Donavon, a 16.2 hh chestnut.

Zoe Jackson Alex's best friend. 14 years old. Sandy hair, freckles. Owns Lace, a 14.1 hh grey.

Camilla Davies Typical Pony Club high-flyer. 15 years old. Owns The Hawk, a 14.2 hh bay.

Judy Richards Ash's head groom and sometime girlfriend. 18 years old.

Eric Burgess Ash's uncle. Around 50 years old. His legs were paralysed in a riding accident. He has a basset hound called Daisy.

Look out for the definition-packed glossary of horsey terms at the back of the book.

CHAPTER ONE

"It's crazy." I stared down at the list of team members for the Pony Club One-Day Event. "It's got to be a mistake!"

Next to my name and Zoe's was Camilla Davies, the most spoilt, arrogant girl you could ever wish to meet. The only good thing about Camilla was her super fast thoroughbred pony, The Hawk.

"It's true." Zoe came off the phone to the Pony Club secretary. "Apparently it's a lesson in public relations. We've all got to learn to get on, team spirit and all that."

"Team spirit my foot, we'll end up throttling each other after a week."

Ever since the last event when my horse Barney had scorched round to take first place, Camilla had been riddled with jealousy. Then I'd started going out with the up-and-coming three-day eventer, Ash Burgess, and she was livid. The livery yard where Zoe, Camilla and I kept our horses was run by Ash for his parents.

"Sparks are going to fly." Zoe ripped open her second bag of salted peanuts.

"Oh no they're not." I thumped down a mug

of steaming tea and accidentally scalded my hand. "Because it's not going to happen. I'm pulling out."

"Alex, you're being completely unreasonable," said Mrs Brayfield, the Pony Club secretary. "Camilla's a lovely girl – once you get to know her."

But that was the trouble. I did know her. She was in my class at school and she kept her horse at the same stables. I could never get away from her.

"Why don't you give it a whirl? You never know, you might become good friends."

"I honestly think there's more chance of me becoming a martian."

"Oh dear. Well, we really would hate to lose you . . . But if that's how you feel, I will have to find someone else to take your place on the team . . ."

"I don't believe it." I switched off Ash's mobile phone in a state of shock. "Zoe, I've agreed to be on the same team as Camilla!"

We pinned the team sheet to the noticeboard in the common room. The one great thing about the Burgess yard was that it came with every amenity. The stables were fantastic wooden loose boxes with rubber matting and automatic waterers, and we had the common room to hang out in – which had everything from a fridge to a dart board and a pool table. Unfortunately the last time I'd tried to play pool, I'd nearly given Judy, the head groom, a black eye.

"I think it's called being stuck between a rock and a hard place." Zoe smoothed out her new powder-blue jods in the mirror. "You know – you're caught in an impossible situation."

The Sutton Vale Pony Club was very short of good riders. The standard was so low that they very rarely competed against other clubs. Instead the team event was made up of teams within the Sutton Vale club, three members instead of the usual four. Our team sheet read:

Zoe Jackson – riding Lace.

Alexandra Johnson – riding Barney.

Camilla Davies – riding The Hawk.

"It could be worse," said Zoe. "We could be landed with Mark Preston."

I pretended to be sick. Mark Preston was the most unappealing male this side of Timbuctoo.

"Speaking of the Preston clan," – I stared out of the window, not sure whether I was seeing things – "look who's coming up the drive."

I would recognize Mark's dad anywhere. Stanley Preston glided into the yard, in his two-tone gold Rolls-Royce with its CC 111 number plate, as if he owned the place. Mr Preston was a business tycoon, or typhoon as we called him, running the *Chunky Chunks* pet food company which was a household name. Mark had once made a curry at school with the *Special Beefy Chunks* and the cookery teacher had given him an A and wolfed the whole lot.

"What can we do for you, Mr Preston?"

He waltzed across to the stables, short, fat and balding and wearing a dark business suit.

"I'm looking for Ash Burgess," he said surveying the yard in one critical sweep. "I want to sponsor him!"

"It's a miracle." I paced up and down nervously.

"It could make all the difference." Zoe was equally wound up. "Why didn't anybody think of him before?"

Mr Preston had been in Ash's office for an hour. Ash had been searching for a sponsor for the past six weeks. He'd already had to sell one of his favourite horses, an ex-steeplechaser with a huge jump. This could be a life-saver.

"What are they doing in there?" I was bursting with frustration.

Judy clattered into the yard on Donavon, who'd been laid off with a leg injury and was only just getting back into work. He was Ash's star horse, a beautiful bright bay with every chance of getting to Badminton.

Judy went dotty when we told her about Mr Preston. Another few months and Ash might have had to sell Donavon. "Do you hear that, boy? You won't have to be sold." She threw her arms round his neck and left a lipstick imprint on his nose.

Mr Preston came out of the office looking stern, got into his car and drove away. Ash came over to the stables, striding along with the sun glinting in his hair. He was wearing the leather flying jacket which I loved and his jeans and chaps. For the millionth time in the last few weeks my heart flip-flopped and I went weak at the knees. "Well, don't keep us in suspense. What did he say?"

"Um, well, the thing is . . ."

"We're listening."

"Well . . ."

"Ash!"

"I've got it! Full sponsorship, feed, vet bills, new horses, new lorry, the lot!"

I was ecstatic. "That's fantastic!" He scooped me up off my feet.

"There's just one drawback. Well, two actually."

"Oh yes?" My feet found the ground with a heady thump.

"All the horses have got to have their names prefixed with *Chunky Chunks*."

"And . . ."

"It's Mark. He's got a new horse. He's going to keep it here – and I've agreed to teach him!"

CHAPTER TWO

"He's awful!" Judy had just had her first glimpse of Mark Preston. "He makes my skin crawl."

He'd swaggered into the yard, an hour late, in tight drainpipe black jeans and Doc Marten boots – dressed more suitably for a rock concert than for a riding lesson. His new horse had arrived earlier in a smart horsebox: a 14.2 jet black cob with a hogged mane. Mark had renamed him Satan and bragged that he was a really difficult ride, that only someone extremely experienced could manage him.

"My niece could ride him," said Judy. "And she's only two years old."

Stanley Preston had promised to deliver specially designed horse rugs and saddle cloths with the *Chunky Chunks* name and logo. Ash was already planning a trip to Ireland to buy a string of new horses and Judy was ringing round for two new showjumping saddles. Ash's eventing career was back on course.

Mark was the only blot on the landscape. He strade out of the common room in starchy white jodhpurs and I tried not to laugh. He looked really uncool. I was leading Barney in from the field with a lead rope made into a halter and Mark's eyes nearly popped out of his head. He even started humming the theme music to Black Beauty.

"So *this* is your star horse!"

A few weeks ago Barney had been in the local paper with the headline: *Wonder horse destined for the top – fought back from the brink of death.*

A couple of years ago Barney had nearly been killed in a horrific car accident. Now he was tipped to be one of the best junior eventers in the country. It was our burning ambition to compete in the National Junior Championships and I was giving myself exactly one year to achieve my goal.

"Not bad." Mark reached out to pat Barney's nose, causing him to pull back.

14.2, Arab/Connemara cross, yellow dun with black points – Barney was striking. Even so, it wasn't like Mark to pay compliments.

He leaned in closer, breathing down my neck. "Maybe you ought to teach me to ride instead of Ash," he sniggered. "You've certainly got better legs."

Ash came out of Satan's stable glowering like a bull.

Zoe had heard Mark too. She came up to me and whispered, "I hate to say this, Alex, but I think Mark's got a crush on you."

"I'd rather kiss a toad." I leaned on the manege railing feeling sick. "He's just trying to make Ash jealous, you know what he's like."

"I know he's got the hots for you, and I know he likes to get what he wants. Watch out, Alex, he could set off World War Three without even trying."

Just the thought of Mark's sloppy rubbery lips on mine made me shudder all over. He was bouncing round the manege trying to show off, legs and arms going in every direction. Poor Satan was doing his best to keep an even rhythm.

Ash was trying to explain to him that he'd got what was known as a "hot seat", meaning that he was tense.

"Well, what am I supposed to do, strap ice cubes to my bum?" replied Mark.

I was just about to go and groom Barney when Judy flew out of Donavon's stable, clutching the radio.

"You're not going to believe this." Her voice had risen to a high-pitched squeak. "It's terrible. What are we going to do?"

Ash bounded across the manege in two strides, his blond hair flopping into his eyes. "Judy, calm down. What is it?"

She put the radio down, fiddling frantically with the aerial. The presenter's voice came over in rapid jerks. "Listen." She grabbed hold of my arm. "Just listen to this!"

A debate was raging on between the presenter and two other men. Someone got through on the phone lines but was immediately cut off. Then there was a female voice: "I can't understand why we need new roads. What about conservation, what about preserving our heritage?"

Mark came over to join us.

"Ssssh." Judy crouched down and turned up the volume.

For the past six months the County Council had been putting forward plans for a new bypass. Ash's parents had been contesting it like mad and Ash had asked me to keep it a secret – if people heard about the risk, they might leave the stables and put them out of business.

"That parkland is beautiful, it's been there for years, some of those trees are the oldest in the county." The woman's voice rose on a wave of emotion. "How can we plough it up to build a concrete bypass?"

"Judy, I don't quite see the point . . ." Zoe was nonplussed.

But I did. Two and two clicked together and made a perfect four. The Burgess property was set in eighty acres of picturesque parkland, with some of the oldest trees in the country.

"Don't you understand?" Judy leapt up, unable to believe that everyone could be so dim. "They've been talking about this bypass for months. But they've just re-routed it!"

Zoe stared at her with dawning realization.

"They're bringing it straight through the stable yard!"

*

"Why didn't you tell me?" I asked.

Ash had collapsed defeated in the common room.

"I didn't even know myself – somebody must have leaked it to the press." He ran a weary hand over his temples and closed his eyes. "We've been fighting this thing for months, Alex. My parents have finally given in. There's no point, they'll do what they want anyway."

"So that's it? You throw in the towel, you let these officials at the town hall dictate your life?" Anger was rushing through my veins. "You can't, Ash. You just can't."

The thought of bulldozers demolishing the stables, all the horses leaving, Ash's business in tatters – it was too much.

"Of course there'll be compensation."

"But this is your home." I spun round, my hair flying all over the place. "Doesn't that mean anything?"

"Of course it does." He stood up, anger in his own eyes now. "I was born here. This land has been in my family for generations. It means everything!"

"Well then, fight!"

"Oh, sorry." Zoe had just come in and suddenly looked embarrassed. "I didn't realize . . ."

Before any of us had a chance to speak, a long, low, blood-curdling scream echoed from the feed room.

"Oh – that'll be Camilla." Zoe couldn't resist a smirk. "She's just found out about being on our team!"

CHAPTER THREE

Zoe and Judy were lying in the sun like a couple of kippers and Camilla had spent the last half hour tacking up The Hawk and applying biscuit-coloured bandages which clashed horribly with his gravy-coloured coat.

"For heaven's sake, Camilla. We're only supposed to be schooling, not meeting the Queen," said Zoe.

She then spent another ten minutes telling me all about a party she'd been to, how her best friend had been so nervous she'd been munching away on a dish of pot-pourri, and how Camilla had snaffled her boy-friend mainly because of the dress she was wearing, which was minuscule and resembled a quilted numnah.

"Is this it?" I said, losing my patience. "I've got one team member who thinks of nothing but food and another who's a raging nympho.

"Lighten up, Alex." Zoe tried to apply coconut suntan lotion and peel a chocolate orange at the same time. "You're far too serious for your fourteen years."

"Well, at least I care," I shot back. "You lot will

still be sunning yourselves when the bulldozers move in."

It was a week since we'd found out about the bypass and hardly anything had been done. I'd organized a meeting of all the horse owners at the yard for the next night but nobody seemed to care one way or the other.

Ash was throwing himself into training a new horse called George with a Roman nose and dished feet, and said his parents were dealing with the objections and it would all sort itself out.

"That's it, bury your head in the sand," I'd yelled. "Typical Taurus, pigheaded and obstinate. I'd rather picket twenty-four hours a day than let all this be dug up. You're a wimp, Ash. You've got no backbone."

I'd stormed out in a steaming temper, having let my mouth run away with me yet again. Even Zoe said I'd gone too far this time.

Ash had disappeared for the whole day, taking Donavon and George to a famous showjumper for extra training. I'd tried ringing his mobile phone but all I got was an engaged tone. I'd have to apologize when he got home.

Barney stumbled into the manege, scuffing through the sand with lazy strides. I concentrated on my position for the first ten minutes, going through a mental drill: chin up, shoulders back, chest out, stomach in, heels down, elbows to the side. Barney snatched at the bit and deliberately ignored my leg.

Camilla clattered into the arena on The Hawk and immediately broke into a canter.

"Haven't you heard of warming up?" I yelled, bristling with annoyance. Horses are like athletes, they need to stretch their muscles gradually, and then build up to peak performance.

"Oh shut up, Alex. You sound more like Eric every day."

Eric was Ash's uncle and probably one of the best trainers in the world. He'd once been a top three-day event rider and *chef d'équipe* of the Olympic team. Then he'd had a terrible riding accident and was now confined to a wheelchair. At the moment he was in Scotland giving a special seminar. He'd left a training programme for me and Zoe but it wasn't the same without him – in fact I felt as if I was falling apart.

"Hey, watch this!" Camilla dug in her spurs and set The Hawk at a massive spread with the top pole at least three foot nine. There was a flurry of sand and flashing legs and then The Hawk, checking back on his haunches because Camilla had put him on a bad stride, soared over the top.

"All this poncy flatwork you do." Camilla pulled up, flushed and smug. "It's not necessary, it's just an excuse to avoid the tough stuff."

"You're talking a load of rubbish as usual."

"I think you're scared."

"I am not."

"Well prove it then. Are you man or mouse? Or is Barney not really that good after all?"

I was livid. And I knew I was playing straight into her hands. Barney had hardly jumped in the manege before and the thick sand pulled at his legs like glue. He'd have to put in a huge effort. The Hawk was fast, agile and light. Barney wasn't used to a short approach.

"*Don't do it.*" Eric's voice rattled in my head.

"Alex, what are you playing at?" Zoe ran across to the gate looking aghast.

I squeezed my legs round Barney's sides and turned for the fence. His head was rammed down into his chest. He wasn't moving forward. He didn't seem to be co-ordinating. We were three strides out. Nothing felt right. I could see Camilla gloating over in the corner. I kicked hard, once, and then again. If things weren't going right you were supposed to keep pushing forward no matter what, keep up the impulsion.

My elbows started flapping. I'd completely lost it. Barney lunged forward, dredging up strength. For a second I thought he was going to take off a stride and a half out. His whole body was screaming out that he didn't want to jump.

"It's OK, boy." I pulled hard on the left rein, desperate to turn him away. The red and white poles loomed up vivid and massive.

"Barney!"

He put on the brakes at the very last minute, ducked his head down and swerved, throwing me off towards the jump.

The force of the pole crashing into the middle of my back made me lose my breath. I was rolling around completely winded, thinking I was about to die. The jump was demolished.

"Alex!" Zoe flew across the sand, just a blur through my streaming eyes. "It's all right, you're just winded."

I tried to ask about Barney, but I could hardly speak.

"He's fine, not a scratch."

The sand filled my mouth. At least I was still alive.

"You idiot!" Zoe rounded on Camilla.

"Don't blame me," she said. "How did I know the stupid nag was going to refuse. He's supposed to be a budding champion according to Eric. I always thought he talked a load of rubbish."

"Barney, you poor baby." I'd got my breath back now. I stumbled across to where he was standing with his huge head hanging down, his eyes so apologetic, so concerned. "It's all right, darling. I'm so sorry."

"Oh please, give me a break." Camilla stuck a finger in her mouth as if to be sick. "Is this something straight out of *National Velvet* or what? Talk about soppy."

"Well, at least we care for our horses," said Zoe. "You just treat them like machines."

"I get results." Camilla dug in her spurs and rode off.

"This is serious, Zoe." I ran my hand down Barney's taut shoulder, feeling the silky smooth skin. My back was breaking in two and tears were dammed up ready to fall at any moment.

"All horses have off days." Zoe tried to disguise her concern.

"Not Barney," I said. "He's never refused in his life." I smoothed down his mane and felt my heart judder in panic. "Oh Zoe, I just know it. Something's terribly wrong!"

The horsebox pulled into the yard with a heavy swish of air brakes. Ash brought Donavon and George down the ramp, one in each hand and took them into the stables. He didn't call Judy once. He just scooped some oats into a bucket and disappeared into George's stable.

"Now's your chance." Zoe patted me on the back so hard that I yelped out in pain. "Peace." She held up two fingers in the victory sign. "Don't blow it."

I'd left Barney in his stable with extra straw bedding and some sliced-up apples. Judy had given him a full examination, taken his temperature, looked in his eyes, felt his legs. Nothing. To everybody in the yard Barney seemed in perfect health.

I picked a marigold from a sad-looking hanging basket and marched with purpose into George's stable.

"Peace," I said, extending the flower. And Ash looked up in genuine surprise.

"It's not that I'm angry with you." Ash bent down and yanked at the velcro on George's travelling boots. "It's just that you're so intense, so dramatic, it's like dating a tornado."

"It's only because I care." My voice hovered between apology and sounding huffy. I desperately wanted a big cuddle but didn't dare ask.

"Can you imagine what it's like at the moment?" Ash stood up as George attacked one of his two huge hay nets. "I've got a sponsor who expects miracles, I've got his son as a pupil who quite frankly rides like a melon and talks like a fool. I've only got one decent horse, I've got a stable yard which is going to be ploughed up and all the owners are pulling out faster than you can say your own name. Then I've got a girlfriend who hurls abuse and storms off like a raging bull."

"I know. I'm sorry." I chewed frantically on my bottom lip, trying to look repentant. "It's just that I believe if you really care about something, you shouldn't give in, not until the end, not ever."

"I agree."

"What?"

"Come here, you passionate creature." He pulled me into his arms. "We'll fight these officials, is that a deal?"

"Yes," I gulped as he planted a big kiss on my forehead.

Meanwhile, George slobbered over his shoulder with a mouthful of hay.

"Ouch," I howled as Ash pressed his hand into the small of my back and leant down to kiss me. "Who's the passionate one now?"

"Order, order!" Ash crashed the walking stick down hard on the table. "Would everybody please be quiet?"

The meeting had turned into a chaotic babble of protests and ridiculous questions. I never knew horsey people could be so troublesome – everybody wanted to talk at once.

Most of the horse owners were present, including a crop of locals from the village. There was a flurry of raised arms as Ash invited more questions.

"Any minute now and they're going to start hitting each other." Zoe was next to me ready to pour out coffees from litre flasks. Ash's mother was handing round spicy vol-au-vents and Camilla was flirting with every man under thirty. I was getting hotter and hotter in a long-sleeved fluffy jumper which looked great but felt like a hair vest. Surely it was only a matter of time before I'd internally combust? Sweat was running down my back and I was terrified in case Mark

Preston put his hand up it. He'd already undone Camilla's bra strap and shocked Zoe with a good luck kiss.

"How dare he?" she'd spluttered. "Even Camilla said she wouldn't let him kiss her."

And then Camilla made Zoe feel worse by adding that Mark was just trying to make me jealous.

"If we could pull together we could make an impact." Ash was flagging badly and failing to drum up an ounce of support.

"Oh yeah? And what if we keep our horses here and they go ahead with the bypass? What if we can't find any other stables?"

"Hear, hear!" Jenny, who owned a hypochondriac thoroughbred called Gypsy Fair nodded her head like a sparrow. I couldn't believe she'd joined the opposition.

"Give the lad a chance," Mrs Brayfield, the Pony Club secretary, called from the back. She stuck out like a beacon in pink wellies and tartan skirt.

"What we need is picketing," someone shouted from the front. "There's nothing like a good stand. Show them what's what."

"That's more like it," said Ash, flushed with enthusiasm.

"Thank God for that." Zoe pushed back her short sandy hair. "I thought they were going to start throwing tomatoes."

Camilla picked up the petition clipboard and waltzed off to chat up some of the villagers.

"So we agree to a demonstration outside the town hall?" Ash winked at me as he warmed to the cause.

I caught a glimpse of my parents arriving with Camilla's mother who my dad always insisted looked like a blonde version of Joan Collins.

"Help." I made an embarrassed plea to Zoe and disappeared under the table to fetch some more cups. The last time my mother had visited the stables she'd insisted she could knit a special blanket for Barney or maybe even crochet a rug, and I'd been completely mortified. The only thing they knew about horses was that Red Rum had won the Grand National three times. But they knew how much I loved riding and had always supported me.

"It's all right, Alex. They're sitting at the back."

Suddenly, Mark Preston burst through the door. He didn't look sober and he was leading the stable's latest resident, a pretty chestnut Shetland pony, only three feet high, with long creamy eyelashes and inappropriately named Goliath – Golly for short.

"Alex, do something!" Zoe was horrified.

"Let not these council clowns be guilty of making little Golly homeless." Mark swayed dangerously and hiccuped extremely close to my parents.

"You trouble-causing fool." Mrs Brayfield brandished her handbag, ashamed that a Pony Club member should make such a spectacle.

Everybody started howling with laughter. Mrs

Brayfield grabbed the lead rope, swivelled Golly round and took him back to his stable.

"What on earth is going on?" A familiar voice boomed out in deep baritone from the open doorway. "Is this a meeting or a school pantomime?"

Ash gave me a look of total relief. The wheelchair crunched heavily down the aisle and stopped next to a silent Mark Preston.

"Is nothing to be taken seriously around here? Well, let me tell you," – the hard flinty eyes scanned the room – "those halfwits at the town hall will dig up these stables over my dead body."

Two stout farmers in the corner whistled their approval.

"This is Burgess land and it's going to remain that way. No matter what. Is that clear?"

"Hear, hear!" Everybody gave a cheer. Zoe even tried to wolf whistle.

Eric Burgess had come home.

CHAPTER FOUR

"The Buccaneers?" Zoe suggested. "Or The Trojans? The Androids?"

We were trying to think of names for our team.

"Robin Hood and his Merry Men," sneered Camilla.

We were having a team training session and Eric was trying to teach us how to jump straight by placing poles in the middle of the fences to form a V shape. The Hawk kept jumping to the left and Camilla was getting more and more infuriated.

"Hadn't you better ask Headquarters," she snapped, meaning Eric. "After all, we're not allowed to make any decisions for ourselves."

But Eric was too busy watching a rickety blue horsebox making its way towards the stables. "Who's that?" he frowned.

"How do we know?" Camilla sniped. "What do you think we are – mind-readers?"

"Less of the cheek, madam, or you'll be off the team."

"Gladly." Camilla struggled to tighten The Hawk's girth while he pressed back his mean little ears and pulled a face at Barney.

Unfortunately I knew exactly who was in that horsebox. And the very knowledge of it made my heart sink.

"I'm so sorry, Ash, but you know how it is." Jenny's voice drifted away, laced with guilt, her hands dithering nervously. "I think it's for the best."

Gypsy Fair reluctantly came out of her stable wrapped from head to foot in protective clothing and resembling an Armadillo.

She was leaving the yard.

"I've no choice." Jenny tried to ease her conscience.

Golly was going too. He tottered out behind Gypsy, all 29½ inches of him. His owners held him as if he were a neurotic racehorse. Poor Golly, he hadn't been quite so pampered since he'd failed to qualify for the Shetland Grand National.

"Well that's that, then." Ash stared down at a filled-in cheque, Jenny's scrawly writing all over it, payment until the end of the month. "If any more horses leave this yard I'm finished." He glanced across to a whole new row of stables which now stood empty, his usually dazzling blue eyes flecked with desperation. "Just who is going to keep paying the bills?"

To add to Ash's worries, Stanley Preston had become a tyrant. He was insisting that Ash enter Donavon for Gatcombe even though there was hardly any time to get him fit.

"There's no way he can do that course." Judy was in tears as she pulled back Donavon's rugs and set to work with the body brush.

Mr Preston had just left in a storming temper, having given Ash a public dressing-down and criticizing the way he ran the yard. Luckily Eric had gone back to his cottage, otherwise the two of them would have ended up in a real head-to-head. "Whatever you do," Ash had said, "don't tell Eric about Preston. He'll blow the whole thing sky-high."

"Look at him, Alex." Judy slapped the muscle on Donavon's shoulder. "It's just flab."

He was such a beautiful horse. He could be a star one day, but not if he was rushed. Not if he was forced to go round Gatcombe.

"Ash can't agree to it." I leaned heavily against the stable wall. "He just can't!"

"He's a moron." Ash clunked a pair of spurs down on the pool table and struggled to take off his boots. He'd just had a phone call while he was in the middle of giving someone a lesson. "Now he's criticizing the feed bills, can you believe it? He won't pay for any extra supplements, says they're a waste of money and that I spoil the horses."

Everybody in the eventing world knew that competition horses had to have expensive diets; lots of vitamins, nothing but the best.

"And there's more," he continued. I'd never seen

him look so trapped. "He wants to set me up in his own yard, no lessons or other people's horses, just eventers... Some might say it's the chance of a lifetime."

"More like he's trying to buy you."

"He's already drawn up a three-year contract."

"Let him find some other mug. You're worth more than that, Ash. Don't sign your life away."

"Yeah, and what's the alternative? Bye-bye, eventing. Bye-bye, any chance of getting to the Olympics? As far as I can see, Alex, I don't have a choice."

So much for Stanley Preston being a guardian angel.

"If I don't sign the contract," – Ash ran his hand through his hair, dark shadows of worry showing under his eyes – "I'll have to sell Donavon. And if I have to do that..." His voice caught with emotion. "If I have to do that, then I might as well pack it all in right now. Because it will be over, Alex. The whole dream down the drain."

I'd never heard Ash sound so disillusioned. He'd always been such a fighter.

"What is it they say?" he said. "It's a hard life and then you die?" He pushed open the stable door and walked off with rounded shoulders and a broken spirit.

My whole heart went out to him. I knew what it was like to want something so much it made you feel physically ill. To live, breathe a dream which never materialized. I'd spent years wanting my own pony, cadging rides wherever I could, saving up pennies from part-time jobs. Barney was my dream and I'd got him in the end. Stanley Preston was Ash's dream and it was all going dreadfully wrong.

"Oh Donavon." I buried my head in his soft thoroughbred neck. "Why does life have to be so cruel?"

"Chicken!" Mark Preston leered at me, his bottom lip hanging down, his hands tightening into fists with obvious annoyance.

I refused to get in his car. He'd recently passed his driving test and had just turned up in the yard in his dad's brand new car, demanding to take me for a spin.

"You'll be in trouble if your dad finds out," I said. "You're not even insured."

"So you're not coming?"

He'd got me trapped in the feed room, his body blocking the doorway.

"I'd rather watch paint dry."

His body visibly bristled, his face darkening with a flood of rage.

"You stuck-up little cow!" In one sweeping movement he made a lunge for my arm and caught my wrist. His fingers clenched tight causing me to gasp in pain. "Mark, let go!"

He pushed me back, and the corner of a metal feed bin jabbed into my back. "Let go of my wrist!"

I yanked away but he squeezed harder. "I could break your arm like a twig," he crowed. "Now you're going to get in my car!"

I scrabbled for the metal feed scoop with my left hand. I was panicking now, fear taking over from shock, my mouth bone dry. "Mark, you're hurting me!"

"Alex!" I heard Zoe call as she ran across the yard. "It's your turn to empty the wheelbarrow."

She bounced in the doorway like a vision from heaven, dabbing at her brow with the back of her wrist. "Is everything all right?"

"Perfectly." Mark let go but still held my eyes. "Alex and I were having a discussion about cars."

His features dropped back into place, bolshy, cocky, the Mark Preston we all knew. A fool but seemingly harmless. Talk about a wolf in sheep's clothing.

"Are you all right?" Zoe peered into my face as I leant back and fought for composure. "Only you've gone as white as a sheet."

I decided to go on a hack. I had to get away, to think, to get things in proportion. And I was still worried about Barney. He'd been fine during the lesson with Eric but afterwards in the stable, he seemed agitated, wound up, not his usual self.

He skittered out of the yard gnawing on the bit but once we were on the soft grass he relaxed and lengthened his stride. Maybe it was all my imagination.

One thing that wasn't was Mark Preston's attack on me. I still shuddered when I thought about it. I'd been pushed around by boys at school but there was something about Mark, some sinister quality. He would have hurt me, I was sure of it.

I couldn't mention it to Ash. One word and he'd throw him out of the yard and his sponsorship would be history. I'd have to keep it to myself, push it to the back of my mind, pretend it never happened.

Barney danced sideways, begging me to loosen the reins so he could have a canter. I let the tension out of my fingers and he shot off down the farm track, clumps of turf spraying up in all directions. The power and speed were wonderful: it felt like nothing on earth. I let my hands move forward just an inch and he surged forward even faster. We understood each other, knew exactly what each other wanted. It was a wonderful, inexplicable bond.

"Steady, boy. Whoa." We popped over a big solid log as if it wasn't even there. I could feel my face breaking into an uncontrollable grin. There was no way anything could be wrong with him. He'd never been so switched on before.

The sunlight broke through a clump of trees and I eased back to walk, flicking my feet out of the stirrups and stretching down into the saddle. It was so lovely to get away from the stresses and strains of the yard. I rode on down the farm track, letting my mind wander, daydreaming . . .

I should have been concentrating.

A pheasant flew up out of the hedgerow, screeching, flapping its wings, right under Barney's nose. All accidents happen in split seconds. And so did this.

Barney brought up his head and forelegs, sprawling back in a rear that would have put most broncos to shame. I didn't stand a chance.

My feet weren't in the stirrups and my reins were like washing lines. I grabbed helplessly at a clump of mane and felt it slip through my fingers. I was going to fall.

I landed on my shoulder and immediately curled up into a tight ball. When you fall you're supposed to try and roll away from the horse's legs to avoid getting kicked. I was so frightened I couldn't move.

For one awful long daunting moment I thought Barney was going to land on top of me. His body towered over me, staggering back to keep his balance. Just when I thought I was history he came back down, stumbled and fell on his side.

"Barney!"

The reins tangled round his legs, lumps of soil and grass stuck to his saddle. Within seconds he was back on his feet, trembling from head to foot, his eyes rolling with panic, his breath rasping. But not injured. Thank God.

The pheasant was gone.

"Are you all right?"

The man looking down on me was in his fifties. His hair was stuck up bushily at each side, one side more than the other. He held out his hand to help me up. He was wearing a monocle.

"Y-yes. Oh. Thank you." I didn't know what to make of him.

I clambered to my feet, my legs like spaghetti. Two falls in as many days was really too much.

"You're a thin little thing to be riding a horse like that." He eyed me up, propping the monocle in his right eye. I'd never seen one before. "Are you sure you're OK?"

"Positive." I felt terrible.

"You shouldn't be out riding by yourself – it's not safe."

I became painfully aware that I shouldn't be speaking to strangers and just wanted to get on Barney and ride away. I clutched the end of my crop defensively. He didn't look like a mass murderer.

"I've just been scouting around," he said, pointing to a load of equipment. "Getting things measured up."

Realization came all at once.

"You're from the council!" I was outraged. "This is private property," I protested, grabbing hold of

Barney's reins. "You shouldn't be here, you're trespassing!"

"What, uh, no—"

I didn't give him a chance to explain. "How could you rip up this beautiful parkland? You're all butchers, the lot of you. It stinks, it really does. I just don't know how you could do it."

"Steady on a minute."

"Don't steady me. If you don't get off this land I'll tell Ash Burgess and he'll phone the police."

I swung into the saddle, steaming with anger that they thought they could waltz in and start marking out the road without our permission.

"Well go on, clear off."

My cheeks were red. I'd been so wound up that I didn't notice the froth dripping off Barney's bit when I went to get on. After all, most horses chewed the bit and created saliva. I hadn't thought it was a big deal. Not then. I hadn't realized it was a symptom of something potentially fatal. Not until it was nearly too late.

CHAPTER FIVE

"Well come on, hurry up. We'll never get there at this rate." Eric was in a fluster.

Camilla was locked in the common room desperately applying talcum powder to her false-tanned face which had turned bright orange. Zoe asked her if she'd been eating too many carrots and I just howled with laughter. Ash was late. He'd insisted on taking Donavon for an early-morning canter and hadn't switched on his mobile phone. We couldn't get in touch with him. Zoe had let Daisy off her extendable lead and was chasing her round the muck heap where she insisted on rolling in fresh manure.

"Please, someone, give me strength." Eric fiddled with his cravat and looked frantically at his watch.

We were due at the Town Hall ten minutes ago.

I snuggled deeper into Ash's leather jacket and tried to pretend everything was fine. Eric's car was piled up with placards and banners and I had the petition in my pocket.

It was a really cold dreary morning, not the kind you'd expect in early summer. Not the kind of morning to go on a protest.

"Camilla, will you come out of there!"

Ash clattered into the yard dismounting in a flying leap and saying his watch had stopped and he'd only had it since Christmas. Daisy was sick all over Zoe's right shoe.

"Right, that's it." Eric pushed his wheelchair round to the driving seat. "We're going. Not in five minutes. Not in two minutes. Now!"

Mrs Brayfield was sitting on the Town Hall steps looking up and down the road. A clutch of villagers were huddled together near the main door chattering away like starlings and failing to notice us struggling to get out of the small Fiesta complete with banners. Zoe was wearing odd shoes.

"This is so embarrassing," Camilla cringed into her designer shirt. But then with a face like a satsuma she could talk.

"Right, come on. Let's get this show on the road." Eric expertly manoeuvred into his chair. "Let's show these interfering busybodies just what we're made of!"

"Save our parkland! Save our trees!"

Mrs Brayfield brayed like a donkey: "No to the bypass!" She let out a tonsil-ripping shriek.

"Who needs an army with her at the helm?" said Ash nudging my elbow.

"Keep marching." Camilla prodded me with her banner, suddenly taking an active interest. She wasn't wiggling her hips for nothing. A van-load of college students had turned up to join in and a bit of a "dish" was hot on her heels. A couple of girls asked for Ash's autograph and I twinged with jealousy.

"Oh dear, I think it's getting out of hand," croaked Mrs Brayfield as a handful of students sat down against the main doors and more followed.

"Where's the petition?" Eric fought his way out of a group of protesters.

"Oh crikey, it's the local photographer," said Zoe. She took off her odd shoes and flung them into a flower bed.

Just when I thought things couldn't get more hectic, Jenny appeared with an armful of flasks. "I'm so sorry about taking Gypsy Fair away," she twittered. "If there's anything I can do . . . I've got coffee and aspirins."

Eric looked grateful.

"Save our parkland! Save our trees!"

"Another two hours of this and I should think the whole town will evacuate," said Zoe, fiddling around with her sock.

"What on earth are you doing?"

She pulled out a squashed Mars Bar. "Mid-morning supplies – I'm starving." She peeled off the wrapper.

Eric and Ash posed with the petition for the photographer and gave an interview. Some officials from inside opened the main doors and looked down their noses at the newly-installed squatters.

"If we're not careful we'll all end up being arrested," Mrs Brayfield shrieked.

It wasn't looking very good at all.

"No to bypass! No to bypass!" Somebody dropped their banner and there was a scuffle of feet and bobbing heads.

Suddenly two policemen crossed the road and headed towards the square – just as a young lad with green hair brought out a spray can and started decorating one of the main windows.

"We're done for," Mrs Brayfield quaked.

"Why does somebody always have to go too far?" Camilla for once talked sense.

"Eric!"

"Alex, could I have a word?" Jenny was suddenly at my side, tugging at my jacket.

"Not now, Jen. I've already had some coffee." I craned my neck to see the police officers seize hold of the green-haired vandal.

"This gentleman says he knows you," insisted Jenny.

"What?" I turned round only half-focused. The wispy unkempt hair was unmistakable. So was the monocle. He held out his hand with a mischievous twinkle in his eye. I glared back.

"This is Professor John Daniels." Jenny introduced him, already swooning like a Barry Manilow fan. "He says he can stop the road."

*

"Why didn't you say something?"

We were back at Eric's cottage trying to recover from the day's ordeal and trying to digest what the Professor was telling us.

Daisy was sprawled on a pile of old *Horse and Hounds* chewing at the toy frog which I'd bought her. Eric was still grumbling that the protest had been a disaster and hadn't helped our cause at all. Ash stared out of the window in a trance.

"So you see, it is possible."

Professor John Daniels wasn't from the council. He was Professor of Archaeology at the local university. And he knew his stuff.

"Roman ruins, eh?" Eric pursed his lips and put his fingers together in a church spire. I could hardly believe it myself.

"But I know this parkland like the back of my hand – I've never seen anything," said Ash, accepting a cup of coffee from Zoe. She then disappeared into the kitchen.

"Yes, but do you know what you're looking for?"

The Professor leaned forward in the best armchair saved for guests, his fluffy eyebrows rising up and down, his hair as wild as ever. The monocle bobbed round his neck like a lucky charm.

"Alex has been calling you the monocled stalker," Ash grinned, causing me to turn bright red.

Zoe came back with a cup of boiled water for the Professor.

"Nothing like hot water to clear the pipes." The Professor banged his chest.

I looked down guiltily at my sludgy black coffee and thought of caffeine.

"All we have to do is find some historic evidence. It'll delay plans for the bypass overnight, most likely kill it altogether." His black, curranty eyes whipped round us all. "I've got enough metal detectors to kit out an army. It's just like using a hoover, nothing to it!"

"But will it work? Will it be enough?" Eric looked sceptical.

Ash clunked down his coffee and stated the obvious. "What have we got to lose?"

The Professor spread out some dirty-looking maps on the floor. Daisy thought it was all a game and plonked herself down in the middle. I pushed her away.

According to John Daniels, there was a Roman road running through the Burgess parkland – it was indisputable. He'd been working on local history for five years. He was convinced.

"Let's find it." Eric banged his hand on the armrest of his chair. "We'll form teams. Work all hours. We've only got one week."

"Triffic." The Professor shook his hand. "Splendid. Just one problem."

"Oh yes?"

"According to my calculations," – he put his monocle in – "the road runs right through your front lawn!"

"He's off his head." Camilla was nothing if not scathing. "There's no way a few old trinkets are going to save this place."

"And what would you know, Miss Clever Clogs? You can't even read the directions properly on a tub of fake tan."

"OK, OK, don't get your knickers in a twist, but there's no way I'm doing any digging." She stalked off.

"This is revolting." Zoe had just knelt on a slug.

We'd decided to waste no time at all and Eric's lawn was already dotted with black holes. He winced every time I dug in the spade. The metal detectors were brilliant. They buzzed like mad at the slightest hint of hidden treasure, but up until now all we'd managed to uproot was an old bedspring and a fifty-pence piece. Nothing remotely Roman.

Ash had to go back to the yard for another meeting with Stanley Preston. The dark shadows under his eyes were becoming a permanent fixture from nights without sleep. I couldn't help wondering if it was too big a price to pay – happiness and freedom in exchange for money and possible success. He hadn't looked himself since the day Preston drove into the yard and made him the offer. What kind of life was that?

"Stay out of it," Zoe warned me. "It's his decision. If he doesn't sign the contract he could end up resenting you. Especially if Donavon has to go."

I knew she was right but it was still difficult. I felt so helpless. Stanley Preston was bad news. I just knew it.

"Uuuh!" Zoe shot backwards, sending a trowel flying and knocking me off balance.

Sticking up in the rich soil amongst the worms was a grotesque washed-out hand with three fingers and a thumb looming out. I shrieked and Daisy came loping across to investigate.

"You silly girl." Eric looked down at the hand, reaching out to touch it. I covered my eyes and thought I was going to be sick. "It's just an old rubber glove!"

Back at the yard Camilla had her feet up in the common room, casually reading a copy of *In the Saddle* and trying to file her nails at the same time.

"Don't take too much off." I couldn't resist bitching. "You might lose your reputation for having claws."

But it fell on deaf ears. She was engrossed in a centre-spread article on poisonous plants and didn't rise to the bait.

"Did you know," she said, "horses can die from

one mouthful of yew? Or that bracken, privet, acorns, foxglove, even rhododendron are poisonous?"

It was the first timc she'd ever shown any interest in horse management.

"Be careful, Cam. Next thing you'll be wanting to learn how to muck out."

"That's funny," she said, screwing up her eyes for a closer look.

"What?"

"Oh. Nothing."

I filled three hay nets at record speed and got hay seeds all down my boots. Camilla's mother came to pick her up in the new Range Rover and waved. Then the yard was empty. Deserted. I presumed Ash was in the house talking to Mr Preston. It was only when I approached Donavon's stable that I heard voices.

"I can't do it." Ash sounded tense, on edge. "It's not right, she'd never forgive me."

"I told you there'd be conditions, and this is one of them. Now fix it." It was Preston, obviously making new demands.

I crouched down outside the door, hardly daring to breathe, but unable to move away.

"Alex deserves to be on that team. She's worked hard."

"She'll get over it. If you know what's good for you you'll get it sorted. Get Alex off the team and Mark on."

I gasped.

"But Mark can't ride."

I didn't hear the rest of the conversation. Nigel and Reggie, the two stable ducks, came paddling across looking for titbits and making enough noise for a whole zoo.

"Ssssh."

But it was too late. The door flew open and Preston appeared. "I could have sworn I heard something."

There was nothing to see. I'd run into the feed room and was pressed up against the wall. I'd avoided being caught by a whisker. Any minute now I was sure to sneeze.

"I must have been imagining it." I could see Preston's polished brown shoes through the gap in the door. He took a swipe at little Nigel who was harmless and didn't have a nasty bone in his body.

Ash's head bobbed down and picked him up.

"Remember what we were discussing." Preston opened his car door. "I'll expect a phone call. Just tell her straight. She's not good enough."

CHAPTER SIX

"He won't do it!" Zoe had come back from Eric's plastered in muck, her sandy hair stuck up like a hedgehog.

"He can't throw you off the team – you're the best rider in it."

"All's fair in love and war," I said gloomily. "If only I'd heard the rest of the conversation."

I hadn't seen Ash for over an hour. He'd gone straight into the house after Preston drove off. We were supposed to be going on a date to the cinema and then on for a pizza. What was he going to do, drop the bombshell with his arm round me in the back row? "Oh and by the way, Alex . . ." He had the power. All he had to do was say I was causing trouble. After all, I had a reputation for being a tearaway.

"Alex, calm down. Getting into a state isn't going to help."

"But I love him, Zoe. And you don't know what he's turned into. He's different. He's sold his soul to Preston. He's behaving like his lapdog."

"You don't know that for sure. Going in all guns blazing is not the answer. Now here, drink this." She passed me a mug of tea so laden with sugar it was almost paste. "Listen to Aunty Zoe. Don't burn your bridges. Wait and see what happens."

"But I'm a nervous wreck," I moaned, dragging a brush though my hair and getting it caught. "How am I going to cope on a date?"

I changed into a short skirt and black top in the common room rather than going home. I'd already arranged to meet Ash at the stables. My parents thought "going-out" clothes should consist of tights thick enough to use as a duvet and skirts long enough to cover even a hint of knee.

Zoe rustled through Camilla's grooming box and produced a spot concealer stick and a hair spray. "That girl has her uses," Zoe said, flicking The Hawk's hairs off the concealer stick and tenderly feeling at one of her own spots. I produced some perfume from my lunchbox and overdid it.

"There, how do I look?"

Zoe wrinkled her freckled nose and gave me the thumbs up. "Although I must say I'd rather cuddle up to a hot-water bottle than a man I can't trust."

"Zoe!"

"Just joking!"

Ash appeared in the doorway.

His face was white, his jaw set rigid. This was it then – he was going to tell me in front of Zoe.

"It's Barney," he said. "He's having some kind of seizure!"

Panic swept through me. If anything happened to Barney I wouldn't be able to carry on. I ran to his stable.

"The vet's on his way. Alex, you can't go in there."

Ash had shut the top door just in case he tried to jump out. The noise inside was incredible. Thrashing, kicking, wild neighing.

"I've got to be with him," I screeched, flinging my arm away from Ash. "Let go of me." I snatched myself free and fiddled desperately with the top lock.

"He's not himself." Ash wouldn't give up. "He could crush you to death."

"Alex, be sensible," said Zoe, terrified.

I flung the top door open and gasped in horror.

He was standing, heaving, at the back of the stable; drenched with sweat, flecked with foam, his eyes roving and wild. He was trembling all over. He didn't recognize me.

"Baby, what is it? What's wrong?" I might as well have been a stranger. My heart practically cracked in two.

Ash grabbed hold of me with both arms and dragged me out of the stable. "Now please, wait until the vet arrives."

"But what is it? What's wrong with him?" I was going crazy. "Can't we do anything?"

Jack Douglas strode into the yard, businesslike and professional, as cool as a cucumber.

"Ash, I'll need your help to examine him. You two stay out here for the moment."

Every ounce of fight had gone out of me. It was the worst, I just knew it. He'd carefully break the news to me and I'd go home with Barney's belongings and that would be that.

"Hang in there." Zoe squeezed my hand, but it just made the tears stream, as I let out huge racking sobs. Barney meant everything to me. He was my life. I couldn't bear it if he died.

Everything had gone quiet in the stable. I put my head on Zoe's shoulder and sobbed. Why? Why me? Why Barney?

The vet came out with Ash, holding a blood sample, the stethoscope round his neck, his face grim.

"Not a very nice sight," he said. "I take it you're the owner?"

My voice seemed to belong to someone else. I was frozen, numb to what was coming next, my ears shutting off the inevitable.

The vet told me to sit down in his car because he said I looked as if I was about to pass out. It couldn't be very nice for him either, I thought. I wiped my eyes and got the back of my hand covered in mascara, and blew my nose on Zoe's tissue. I took a deep breath and told him to tell me everything.

"Your horse was suffering from severe convulsions, incoordination, muscle tremors – his nervous system has been overstimulated by a foreign substance."

"Oh."

"I've managed to sedate him. He'll need a few days' total rest, nothing but bran mashes, lots of nursing."

"But . . . I don't understand."

"I think we've caught it in time."

"You – you mean he's all right?"

"I can't totally guarantee it, but I think he'll pull through."

"I thought you were going to tell me that—"

"It's still very serious. I hate to tell you this, Miss Johnson, but your horse has been poisoned."

It was deliberate. Jack Douglas was going to have the blood sample tested but he was pretty sure what had caused it. There was some incriminating evidence by the stable door near the water bucket – slug bait.

"It's lethal stuff. In large doses nearly always fatal. Your horse has been very lucky. He must have nine lives."

None of the other horses in the yard were affected. It was just Barney who'd been singled out.

"But what kind of person would do that?" I couldn't even begin to comprehend. "We haven't seen any strangers around."

"It might be someone right under your nose. Be careful – whoever it is might strike again."

"Can I see him now?" My legs were weak.

Ash opened the stable door and I saw Barney laid out on the straw, his head back, heavy with sedative. His eyes were half closed. The bed was all screwed up from all the thrashing around. I'd fix it later. Make him really comfortable. For now I knelt down beside him, the straw prickling my knees, running my hand gently along his neck. How could anybody want to murder such a beautiful brave horse? It could be a random attacker, a horse hater, or it could be a personal vendetta. Stanley Preston sprang to mind. He had the motive.

"I'm not leaving him." I shrugged off Ash's hand on my shoulder. "He knows I'm here, he needs me."

"OK, but I'd better ring your parents, let them know what's going on."

As soon as he went out of the door I put my arms round Barney's neck and hugged him. I never wanted to go through a scare like that again. Never.

My parents were really good. They brought a blanket and a flask of vegetable soup; one of my Agatha Christie books and my Walkman. Despite trying to get me to go home they at least understood why I had to stay. Ash reassured them he'd keep an eye on me. By ten o'clock Barney lifted his head and managed to prop himself up on his shoulder. He was looking better.

Ash came in ten minutes later. "I've just been on

the phone to Eric. He'll be over tomorrow morning. He says keep your chin up. Barney's a fighter."

"What's in the bag?" I whispered so as not to disturb Barney who was yawning and laying his head back on the straw. His eyes and gums were still unhealthily pale.

"Ground charcoal." Ash put it next to me. "Eric said mix some in with the bran, and it'll soak up any poison still in his stomach. An old remedy."

Unfortunately horses can't be sick like cats or dogs so anything in their system has to stay there. Jack Douglas had considered trying a stomach pump but he really didn't think there was enough slug bait in his system. Thankfully.

"Here, do you want some soup? I've had enough." The steam was making my nose run. My eyes were swollen up from crying and the eye shadow and black kohl were really irritating them. Ash sat down next to me and held my hand.

"I think you're very brave," he said, kissing each of my knuckles very gently. His blue eyes looked almost grey in the shadows. "I also think you're very beautiful."

He kissed me again but I pulled away. "Don't."

How could I kiss a man who might not be loyal, who could be scheming behind my back, putting his career first? He hadn't mentioned a word about the team. I had to have one hundred per cent loyalty.

That's what mattered most: reliability, friendship, honesty.

"Do you want me to go?"

"If you don't mind."

The pain in his eyes was obvious but I looked away. The hurt in my heart was far greater. I needed to be alone.

It's funny how you never really appreciate something until you nearly lose it. I'd always imagined Barney to be there. Invincible. As solid as a rock. But now I felt I was skating on thin ice. Nothing was that permanent. Anything could happen at any time.

I shuddered and pulled the blanket closer round my shoulders. It was going to be a long night.

A Land Rover pulled into the yard at a quarter to midnight. I'd never been so happy to hear Zoe's voice. She came into the stable with her own sleeping bag and a hand muff. "I couldn't sleep," she said. "I couldn't rest with you out here by yourself. You're my best pal. You need me."

Her mother told us to sleep tight and said she'd be back in the morning.

Zoe sat down next to me and pulled out a flask of hot chocolate.

We sat there with our mugs, watching Barney twitching as he slept.

"We've got to talk about it." Zoe finally broke the silence. "We've got to find out who did it."

"I know."

The list of suspects was longer than I imagined. Stanley Preston at the top. Mark Preston. Any owner who might have been in the yard between 3.30 and six o'clock. That's the time Jack Douglas thought the poison had been administered.

"I hate to say it, but there's also Ash," Zoe said. I winced. "And then there's the professor."

"Where do we draw the line?"

"And don't forget the vet thought Barney had been given poison for a few days, which is why you thought he was off colour. I guess that rules out the professor. Barney was ill before you met him."

"What about Camilla?" I said in a grave voice. "She was going on about poisonous plants. Getting quite a buzz out of it. She'd do anything to see me come a cropper."

"Yeah, but she's not a killer. She's spiteful and a pain but she wouldn't go that far. Surely?"

"I wouldn't say Ash was a killer but you've still got him on the list. No, Cam is a definite possibility. You know how she has to be top dog."

"Maybe whoever it was didn't mean to do Barney in, just put him out of action so that he'd miss the team event."

"Let's face it, Zoe," I said, my whole body aching with exhaustion, "the way people come and go out of this yard – it could be anybody!"

CHAPTER SEVEN

Barney made an incredible recovery. The vet arrived at 7.30 a.m. and said he must have the constitution of a rhinoceros. Whoever the poisoner was, they hadn't given Barney enough. Their ignorance had saved his life.

He was still tottery on his legs, but I knew he was going to be all right. He was already getting up to his old tricks, picking up the yard brush with his teeth, butting a football round the stable, generally acting the goon. If he kept on improving like this he'd be fine for the team event.

Jack Douglas, Eric and Ash were in deep conversation. I led Barney back into his stable with Zoe's help and dreamt of steaming scrambled eggs and crisp bacon. Then they told me their idea.

"No, it's too dangerous. I won't let you do it."

Eric took hold of my hand and begged me to think it through. "It's the only sensible option. There's thousands of pounds worth of horse flesh in this yard. You wouldn't want anything to happen to Donavon would you, or George? Think about it, Alex, please."

"I have, and it's too dangerous."

Jack Douglas took over. "We've got to lure the

poisoner into the open. He or she has got to be caught. We've got to use Barney as bait."

"And put his life at risk?" I didn't like the idea one little bit.

"We'll protect him. There'll always be somebody standing guard. I give you my word nothing will happen to him."

Zoe suggested it was a good idea. Ash glanced at me with heartbreaking warmth. "Your word had better be good," I said, "because it doesn't look as if I've got any option."

Zoe and I went home to clean up while Eric held the fort. I was really touched when my mother gave me a Get Well card for Barney with a mint stuck inside. She was so soppy it was embarrassing.

After a shower, a clean set of clothes and two slices of burnt toast I felt able to face the world. My bones were creaking but at least the sun was making an appearance and it looked at last like being T-shirt weather.

Zoe had blow-dried her hair (which stuck up in sandy tufts), applied orange lipstick and blue mascara and still managed to stop off at the newsagent's to buy a magazine.

"Ash has something to tell you," she squeaked, as soon as I arrived back at the yard. "It sounds important."

Judy was lunging George in the arena and a

couple of horse owners were getting ready to go out on a hack. Everything looked perfectly normal. One little girl who had weekly lessons pulled at my coat and asked me where she might buy a horse sock. She'd just adopted a pony from a horse sanctuary and it stated quite clearly that he only had three white socks. A smile came to my lips and I suddenly felt light-hearted and more able to cope. It could only get better. Things couldn't get any worse.

I gave Nigel a handful of oats and patted his feathery little body. He'd taken to sitting outside Donavon's stable and squawking at any passers-by. Zoe said he must think he's a Rottweiler and I just wished he'd stand sentinel outside Barney's stable. After all, that's where we needed all the help.

Ash was just reaching for the milk from the fridge when I walked into the common room. He made me a coffee automatically without asking.

"I've just been down to the Chunky Chunks pet store," he said. "On the outer circle road."

"Yeah, I know where it is."

Instinctively I folded my arms across my chest and became wary. The tension between us was hard to ignore. For two people who could talk their heads off, conversation had suddenly become very difficult.

"I spoke to three assistants," he said, getting straight to the point. "They all verified that Mark had been working there all afternoon from one o'clock until 5.30. There's no way he could have got here in time to poison Barney."

I sat down heavily on a plastic chair. I hadn't told anybody about my run-in with Mark Preston but the mention of his name still made me feel sick.

"We'll have to look elsewhere for our mystery attacker. It seems Mark's got a watertight alibi."

"Yes, doesn't it."

I got up to go out, desperately needing a waft of fresh air.

"Alex, if something's wrong, you will tell me, won't you?" His eyes looked sad. "Oh and I nearly forgot. Eric wants you all together for a team training at eleven. Mark Preston's cancelled his lesson so I said you could ride Satan."

"Fine. I'll do that."

Satan, it turned out, was as far from being a demon as you were ever likely to get. Zoe said he'd belonged to someone in the Pony Club and his original name was Snowball. He was so sweet, he didn't put a foot wrong. He was one-paced and he tended to lean into the inside rein, but apart from that he was a little treasure. It just showed how pathetic Mark was at riding.

Eric told me to push him into canter and I tried to get him to bend round my inside leg, but he was as stiff as a board. "It's all right, boy, just do your best."

Camilla was already moaning her head off that

we'd done too much flatwork and that was after only ten minutes of circles and transitions.

Eric was in a mood because he couldn't push his wheelchair through the sanded arena and Ash had to help him. Usually we trained over at his cottage but I didn't want to let Barney out of my sight for a second. Zoe was slouching around on Lace obviously a million miles away and Daisy was tied up to the gate post digging a hole big enough to stage *The Great Escape*.

"More leg, Camilla, for heaven's sake. You've got as much style as a slug on a plastic lettuce." Eric was running out of patience fast.

The Hawk for once had his nose tucked in and was moving in a rhythm. Camilla was scarlet in the face but determined not to give in.

"Count out a rhythm," Eric bawled. "One hundred, two hundred, three hundred. Slower, slower, now change the rein."

Zoe came back to planet earth with a bump when Lace shied at a jump stand and Zoe went sprawling up her neck.

"Diabolical," Eric shouted.

Zoe smiled apologetically and then managed a lovely working canter. Lace was a really good dressage horse when Zoe put her mind to it.

When Eric put down some trotting poles, Satan was completely baffled and did a flying leap over all of them. Camilla was mortified when Eric asked Ash to tie her thumbs together with baler twine. She really thought it was a wind-up. I'd once had to ride with my thumbs tied together for two whole days.

"If you insist on riding with your hands all over the place, what do you expect?" Eric was enjoying every minute.

"It's outrageous! Untie me immediately. I can't steer."

The Hawk, taking full advantage, went cannoning off to chat up Lace, and Camilla lost a stirrup and started screaming.

"A one-legged fairy scared of heights could ride better than you lot," Eric grunted. "And Alex, it's no good being able to just ride Barney to perfection. If you want to be an eventer, you've got to ride more than one horse."

Satan, sweating and out of puff, came to a grinding halt in front of a two-foot-six jump. Camilla bounded back across the arena, clutching at the reins. The Hawk stopped in front of Satan and pulled a face.

"Oh cripes, what's this?" Zoe pulled up from trot, her mouth dropping open.

The motorbike that roared into the yard was unlike anything I'd ever seen. It was a monster machine. If I'd been on Barney he'd have bolted and I'd have been at Land's End by now.

Ash was awestruck. "It's a Harley Davidson," he drooled. "A real life Harley Davidson."

That could have been a Hollywood film star for all I knew about bikes. It was fantastic though. It had huge headlights and a windshield and throbbed like a racing car. Whoever was riding pillion was wearing ribbed tights, brogues and carrying a British Home Stores carrier bag.

"Isn't it wonderful?" Jenny ripped off her helmet and clambered off. "I've had the time of my life." Her cheeks were glowing pink and her hair suggested she'd just been skydiving.

The Professor took off his own helmet and shook Ash's hand. "Fine woman, that." He pointed to Jenny. "Hangs on like a limpet. Picked her up at the bus stop. Never looked back since."

Jenny blushed and passed Eric a jar of her home-made lemon curd. Ash was already asking about engine sizes and valves and drooling like a little boy. "Never mind about the bike," the Professor said. "I'm here to sort out these Roman ruins. Time's running out fast."

"Oh JD, you're so masterful," said Jenny. She looked twenty years younger. I presumed JD stood for John Daniels.

"What were you saying, Camilla," I whispered, "about the Professor being a stuffy old bloke?"

She stuck her tongue out and marched off to the stables with The Hawk, rubbing at her hands as if she'd undergone some medieval torture.

"Did that young man find what he was looking for?" Jenny rubbed at her knee and beamed at me with a megawatt smile. "A back protector or something. I told him to ask you."

"Jenny, I don't know what you're talking about."

"I came up to the yard yesterday, about five o'clock, just to say that I was bringing Gypsy Fair back – I should never have taken her away in the first place. There was this man rooting about, looking for something."

We all went silent.

"Was he in his forties, shortish, a bit aggressive, wears a hairpiece?"

"Oh no, half that age," she went on. "Quite tall, didn't say much. Asked me not to say anything because he was going to surprise you."

"Could you identify him?" My heart was somersaulting. "You see, I think you've just described somebody I know. Somebody I really need to talk to. His name's Mark Preston."

The shop assistants must have been lying. Zoe produced a school photo with Mark in the sixth-form row and bingo, Jenny was on to him straight away. It was him all right. I was all for finding him right now, challenging him on the spot.

"No, Alex, we don't have a scrap of evidence. Let's let him make the next move." How could I for one fraction of a second have ever thought it could be Ash?

Barney adored having so much attention. He

stood in his lovely thick straw bed drinking weak tea with three sugars poured into a plastic saucer. I'd bandaged his legs to keep him warm and lovingly made up a bran mash and left it to steam. Jenny suggested seaweed from the local health store, but I gave it a miss. Gypsy Fair must rattle with every concoction available to man and beast.

"If he doesn't show tonight I think we ought to go to the police," said Ash, genuinely worried.

"Here it is!" Camilla fished the *In the Saddle* mag out of the bin and pointed to the centre-spread article.

There was a sub-title, *Garden and Domestic Poisons*. Slug bait was mentioned.

"Now we know where he got the idea from," I said through gritted teeth.

"It makes me feel queasy just thinking about it." Zoe put a hand on her stomach.

I went to help Ash do evening stables, checking hay nets and water, sweeping up any loose straw. I was tingling with a mixture of anger, outrage, anticipation and a strange kind of exhilaration. My mind was racing.

"Alex." Ash looked over Barney's door where I was just fixing his rug. The Get Well card was pinned up in the window. "There's something I've got to tell you, about Stanley Preston – about the One Day Event . . ."

He didn't have to say any more. His eyes spoke

volumes. He'd done the right thing and relief surged through every vein in my body. Slowly the cogs in my head clicked together. The idea started to take form. It was perfect. The ultimate coup.

"I've just had the most brilliant idea!" I grabbed hold of his arm and dragged him towards the house. "We've got to find Eric – there's not much time!"

CHAPTER EIGHT

The darkness was all-embracing. Just the steady rustle of horses shifting position, the straw tickling in the small of my back. I clutched on to Ash's hand and rubbed my thumb against his. We were crouched in the far right-hand corner of Barney's stable, hardly daring to breathe. There wasn't a single light on anywhere – we couldn't even see the time.

I was terrified. It was only having Ash next to me that kept me sane. He was after all every girl's dream bodyguard. "If this wasn't so frightening it could almost be romantic," I whispered, smothering a giggle.

I pulled my knees up to my chin and wrapped my arms round my legs. We could be here for hours and maybe for nothing. Would he turn up or wouldn't he? I pulled strips off a blade of straw. Yes he will, no he won't, yes he will . . . An owl hooted somewhere in the parkland. It must have been nearly midnight.

"What was that?" Ash suddenly stirred beside me.

"What? I didn't hear anything." Small tremors of panic raced up and down my spine.

"It's a loose horse!" Ash sprang up as the clattering hoofs skidded on smooth concrete. One of the stable doors swung open. "It's Donavon!"

I couldn't move. I couldn't talk. I just stood trembling from head to foot as Ash raced out of the stable. Barney's shadow stirred behind me. And something else. Another shadow flickering on the far wall. Somebody was outside. Somebody was outside the door and it wasn't Ash. A steady trickle of sweat ran down my back. *Oh God, please help me.*

An arm appeared and reached for the top bolt. "Come on, boy, it's time to take your medicine . . ."

The familar spongy, pock-marked face loomed up in the dark. Oh he thought he was so clever, using Donavon as a decoy, getting Ash out of the way. But he didn't expect me. He didn't expect his evil little plan to backfire.

"No!" I yelled, smashing my whole body weight against his. "Get out!"

"Hey!" He jumped back surprised, something in his right hand clattering ominously into the gutter.

"You pig!" I yelled, anger washing over me, drowning the white-hot fear. "You pig, you pig!" My hands battered against his chest.

"Belt up!" He slapped a cold clammy hand over my mouth and twisted my arm sickeningly behind my back. "Now be quiet, you little cow. Just shut it."

I could feel his heavy hot breath on my neck, his groping hand round my waist. "Now come on, you're coming with me."

Panic rose inside me. Where was Ash? Where was Mark taking me?

"That's better," he leered as I stopped struggling for a moment. "All we need to do is talk. You'll soon come around." He planted his fat lips in a sludgy kiss on my temple, and revulsion made me yank away in horror.

"Now now, don't get stroppy." His voice dropped to a tender note. "I just want to talk, that's all."

His hand relaxed a little where it had been digging into my ribs. I knew this was my only chance. Swivelling my body round until I thought my arm would break I heaved up my knee and whacked him in the groin.

He doubled up, stepping back, almost drunkenly, anger erupting on his face. Then he pushed me against the stable wall, the hard brick cracking into the back of my head.

"All you care about is that flaming horse," Mark glowered. "Barney this, Barney that – what about me? Don't you care anything about me at all?" He lunged forward intent on trying to kiss me.

"Leave her alone." Relief made my knees almost buckle.

Ash stepped out of the shadows, his face cold with rage. "If you ever touch her again . . ." He grabbed at Mark's collar and shook him until his eyes goggled. "You miserable bullying worm." I'd never seen Ash so angry: his eyes glittered, the muscles in his neck stood out. He put his hand into his pocket and pulled out a hypodermic syringe. "I believe this is yours – you dropped it outside the stable." Ash held it up in the dim moonlight and Mark crumpled with fear.

"Don't tell my dad, whatever you do. Please don't tell him."

"You'll be lucky." Ash glared with burning contempt. "I'm going to phone him right now."

The CC 111 gold Rolls Royce edged into the yard at twenty past twelve. The light was on in the common room. Ash was pacing up and down and Mark was huddled in a heap, frantically chewing at his thumbnail. I sipped at a cup of tea and gradually felt shock receding.

Stanley Preston stormed through the door bristling with anger. "This better be good, Burgess. I don't come out in the middle of the night for nothing."

Mark jumped visibly. "Hi Dad, I – I can explain."

Stanley Preston stared straight through his son and then glared at Ash. "What the hell is going on?"

Ash told him the facts, straight up, without any emotion. Then he took the hypodermic syringe off the pool table and squeezed out a few drops of the menacing white liquid. "Bleach," he said, "one hundred per cent concentrate. It burns the mouth and stomach, making the horse really ill and unable to eat."

"I didn't mean it." Mark slumped back in his chair. "I didn't realize, Dad, honest."

"You stupid, stupid fool." Preston loomed over him as if about to lash out. "I told you I'd get you on that team – you're too thick to handle anything yourself." Mark scraped his chair back, genuinely startled at his Dad's aggression. "You foolish little milksop. Get in the car. Go on, here's the keys. Get out of my sight."

Mark grabbed the keys and left as fast as he could.

"And as for you," Preston turned back to Ash, his eyes narrowing into tight slits, "I'm going to make you work hard for your sponsorship money."

"I think not." Eric took his cue and wheeled out from behind the fridge. His voice was level, cutting and totally in control. "You see, Mr Preston, I think this time we've really got you sewn up."

Preston's mouth dropped open and closed without a word as he saw the tape recorder on Eric's lap. He took a step backwards, stunned and caught off guard.

Eric pressed the stop button on the tape recorder and pulled a sheet of A4 paper out of a brown envelope. "Luckily my solicitor managed to draw this up at a moment's notice. I trust it will be to your liking. It cancels all contracts we have with you."

Eric gently proffered the document and Preston snatched it out of his hand and read it at lightning speed. Eric winked at me and I burst into a winning smile.

"Dream on, old boy." Preston flung the document down on the pool table.

"Oh come now, Mr Preston, let's think this through. Do you want your son splashed all over the papers as a horse molester or would a quiet police caution be better? They should be with us shortly to arrest him."

Panic contorted Preston's face. "How could you?"

"Oh believe me, with great pleasure." Eric gave him an eyeball-to-eyeball glare which would have put the frighteners on even the most hardened criminal.

The document lay on the table, curling up slightly at the edges.

Preston was livid. His face turned from stark white to pink. His jowls quivered like an overweight bulldog.

"And in case you've any difficulty making up your mind," Eric continued, "there's always the case of your doling out backhanders to the council. I've been doing a bit of checking up on you. It suddenly struck me, you see, that you actually want Ash out of this yard. You want to have total control."

I didn't know that was coming. Ash shot me

a look of pure amazement and I just shrugged my shoulders.

"You've got no proof." Preston was on the run now, floundering, his hands were even starting to shake.

Sock it to him, Eric. I felt like giving him a bear hug.

Preston fumbled for a pen. "I'm warning you, Burgess, you won't get away with this. I'll have the last word." He grabbed the paper and swirled in his signature – on the dotted line. Ash and I were witnesses.

"It's been nice doing business with you." Eric gave him a thin smile.

"You're going to regret you ever pulled one over on me." Preston was livid. "I'll get my own back," he said marching across to the door. "I'll ruin you, Burgess, just you wait and see." His voice was drowned out by the sound of sirens as the police arrived and took Mark away.

Silence fell. All we could hear was a moth battering around the overhead light bulb.

"I can't believe it's worked." Ash's voice sounded strained. He picked up the document and stared at the signature for reassurance. I felt weak with tension. Eric slumped, suddenly grey and exhausted.

"You were fantastic." I genuinely meant it.

"Like the Godfather," Ash grinned, patting his uncle on the back.

"I don't think Mark will be trying to nobble any more horses," I said.

"Though he'll probably be let off with a warning," Eric sighed.

"All we need now is a new sponsor." I turned to Ash. "Are there any letters you haven't had replies to?"

"One or two," he said. "I'll chase them up in the morning."

Ash came into the yard the next day with Zoe's father, Mr Jackson.

"Come and meet my new sponsor," he called.

"B-but how?" I was totally amazed.

"I wrote to Mr Jackson a few months ago, but he never got the letter," said Ash. "His company is going to sponsor me for the next year!"

After Mr Jackson had left I told Zoe all about Mark and his father, in confidence.

"He's rich, powerful, nasty and out for revenge." She made it sound like some kind of television soap saga.

"Remember, Zoe, not a word to anyone."

"What do you think I am, Motormouth of Britain?" She tugged at one of her curls and pursed her lips. "But you've got to admit, it's the best bit of gossip ever."

I plonked myself down exhausted in an old armchair and Nigel came waddling in with a grease mark over one wing where he'd been squeezing under the horsebox. I fed him a marmite sandwich and tried to stifle a yawn.

Ash and I had been so happy the night before that we'd talked for hours about the future: Donavon, George, Barney, Badminton, the National Championships, fame, recognition. We knew that for both of us to become world-class eventers it was going to be a long, hard haul, but every second would be filled with excitement. It was the challenge – the achievement.

"We've got to win this team event," I said to Zoe. "I've got to show that creep Preston."

I'd not felt right since Ash had told me what Mr Preston said about Barney: that he was the ugliest nag he'd ever seen and he'd be better off pulling a rag and bone cart.

Barney was no show horse but he could jump the side of a house. He was a star.

"Oh dear." Zoe slapped a hand on her forehead. "I recognize that tone of voice – the girl means business."

"Too right I do." I whisked Nigel up and plopped him on my lap.

"We're going to win that trophy even if I have to brainwash Camilla and ban you from ever eating chocolate again. Motivation, determination and dedication. That's all we need."

"And talking of Camilla pulling her weight . . ."

She stood up, looking out of the window, and raising a high arched eyebrow. "Just take a look out there."

It was raining in a thin misty drizzle, which was why we were holed up inside. The Hawk was gracefully executing a figure of eight in the arena, a picture of intense concentration, Camilla purple in the face and ramrod-stiff with effort.

Best of all, Eric was rattling out instructions from under his umbrella, getting them turning this way and that without the slightest lip from Camilla.

"He's finally broken her spirit," I said in total awe. "Is that really the Camilla we know and love?"

CHAPTER NINE

"Legs, legs, legs, more inside rein. Come on, put your back into it." Eric was in his element.

It was raining again. Zoe had her shoulders hunched up to her ears, and Camilla looked barely recognizable, with her hair in damp clumps and mascara leaking all over the place.

As the rain bucketed down in relentless sheets Eric directed Zoe, who was riding a twenty-metre circle more like an oval.

"Look ahead," he bawled. "Where's your posture?"

I was buzzing with elation and flashing everyone a neon smile. It was the first time I'd ridden Barney since his recovery and he was positively vibrating with energy. His long powerful legs stretched out at a working trot and his coat glistened and rippled like rich oil. I was only allowed to walk and trot but it was obvious he'd made a fantastic recovery. He was fighting fit.

We had an audience of a couple of mothers who'd booked in lessons with Ash and who were both frantically trying to pacify a screaming four-year-old called Jessica with packets of crisps.

"Did you know Jessica means 'God beholds'?" Zoe rode up, rubbing at her nose with a drenched tissue. I was just about to give a glib answer when Eric called us into the middle.

Camilla was doing fantastically well. She was about to tackle a row of jumps consisting of a bounce and a stride to an upright, and then two strides to a spread.

"Ride deep into the corner," Eric shouted. "Keep him on a short stride."

I was so busy thinking of hot Bovril and waterproof clothing that I didn't notice Barney chewing Eric's umbrella.

The Hawk was a changed horse. He usually took every jump at a hundred miles an hour, showing amazing talent but not much control. He was as fast as a Porsche but without the brakes, and so in the showjumping he often flattened the last combination.

Eric was showing Camilla how to get him back on his hocks, get him thinking and pinging his fences, lifting his shoulders. He was improving by the minute.

"If we carry on like this, we could even win." Zoe slouched in the saddle and earned a disapproving look from Eric.

"The most important thing is to keep a rhythm and not get rattled when things go wrong."

Eric had shown us endless video clips of Mary Thompson riding King William and keeping as cool as a cucumber no matter what.

"I'm a redhead," Zoe sulked. "How can I possibly be expected to stay cool?"

Luckily Lace was as good as gold and wouldn't know the meaning of "napping" despite constant demonstrations from Barney.

Eric was just about to give us a lecture on safety and the importance of properly fitted back protectors when Zoe's eyes glazed over. This meant she was on the verge of a brainstorm.

"The Trailblazers," she said, almost breathless. "That's what we'll call our team."

Camilla gave her a deadpan stare. "Well, it could have been worse," she said. "It could have been the Three Little Foxes."

"Or the Three Little Bears," I giggled.

"Well at least you finally *all* agree on something," said Eric.

Maybe team spirit wasn't in such short supply after all.

The Trailblazers had never worked so hard in their lives. Two days before the event we could barely move, let alone ride a cross-country course. My muscles felt as if they'd seized up completely and Zoe was complaining of a bad back.

The rain was never-ending. Mrs Brayfield was having palpitations as to whether she might have to cancel, and Eric had the blacksmith out to Lace,

Barney and The Hawk to fit stud holes for extra grip. It was all getting very professional.

The atmosphere in the yard was tense. It seemed inevitable that plans for the road were going to go through. There was a committee meeting at the town hall the next afternoon and it seemed a foregone conclusion.

The Professor was wracked with guilt at having got our hopes up for nothing. Eric's garden looked like an army of moles had attacked it, but nobody had the heart to do anything about it. Ash's parents were talking about buying a piece of land on the other side of town, and putting up some loose boxes and converting a barn into a flat for Ash. Luckily their house wouldn't be pulled down, but looking out over a bypass wasn't a very nice prospect.

Doom and gloom spread like a blanket of fog. Ash came into the common room shaking out his riding coat and complaining about an owner who had "barbed wire round his wallet".

George won a novice event, which went completely to his head and he had to be moved into a different stable with a stronger door. He and Donavon seemed to be in competition with each other for the "star horse" of the yard. Ash said George was a good second string but every now and then he'd switch off and behave as if he was stupid.

Camilla was complaining of physical and mental exhaustion while wildly backcombing her hair and applying black nail varnish which she said aptly reflected the mood.

Eric was throwing himself into the team event almost as if it was the only thing he could positively do something about. None of us wanted to face the prospect of bulldozers and miles of concrete. It was easier to bury our heads in the sand.

Eric arrived at lunchtime with a lecture board borrowed from the professor, a boot-faced expression and three flaming red rugby shirts emblazoned with *The Trailblazers*.

That morning we'd given the horses a two-mile canter and then some hillwork which made my pectorals feel as if they'd been ripped apart. Then we'd dutifully washed their manes and tails and Cam had insisted on using some spray-on "Shine Coat". This had streaked and we'd ended up having to bathe The Hawk from head to hoof, which completely stripped his gravy-coloured coat of any remaining oil.

Eric thumped up the ramp into the common room, looking in no mood for complaints. He was wearing his navy checked tie and engraved cufflinks, which always meant he was in one of his "power" moods. Daisy curled up under the pool table, surreptitiously gurgling into one of Ash's leather boots.

"This is the start." Eric drew in a line on the board with a felt-tip pen. "This is the first, just straw bales, two foot ten, onto the tyres which have a nasty take-off; you've got to aim left and stay left – the coffin comes up all too fast."

Eric always said that to ride a good course you had to memorize every stride, every blade of grass. He was meticulous in details about the approach, what best line to take, and hammered us with questions until he was blue in the face.

None of us expected what he threw at us next. Fence number nine was a Normandy bank. Zoe mouthed like a goldfish and I froze. A Normandy bank was a huge mound of earth with a flat top which you had to jump on and off. I'd once seen a rider on television do a flying dive and end up in a crumpled heap. It was usually the kind of obstacle seen at affiliated events.

"Mrs Brayfield wanted to liven things up a bit." Eric gave a twisted smile. "Inject some variety."

"She's certainly done that," I squeaked. "Nobody will get any further – there'll be a pile-up!"

"I can't do it." Zoe nearly slithered under the chair. "It's suicidal."

"You can and you will." Eric was unrelenting. "Zoe, you'll go first, then Camilla, and last Alex. It's up to you, Zoe, to report back to the others."

Zoe's freckles seemed to be standing out in a hot haze of panic. "And remember, it's not good enough to be very good, or even excellent. You've got to be the best."

*

"Just keep on a short bouncy stride – think of it as jumping an upright. And lean back when you jump off."

It was all right for Ash to say. He'd jumped more Normandy banks than he'd had hot dinners. He wouldn't be there when I was launching myself into space.

We'd decided to take Daisy for a walk, mainly because she'd been so badly behaved even Eric couldn't cope with her. The heavy leaden sky had cleared slightly and pink rays of sunshine poked nervously through the clouds. I suddenly remembered geography lessons and all about mackerel cloud formations, only I couldn't remember any more because I'd been too busy drawing a picture of my dream horse on my geography text book.

Daisy snortled through the damp, dirty leaves, her tail arched over her back, her ears shuffling along the ground. Ash showed endless patience as she sniffed out rabbits and picked up wet sticks. I crumbled a handful of horse nuts in my pocket and felt a huge heavy weight settle in my chest. Ash stalked along in silence, his wide sultry mouth pulled in with tension. He hunched up the collar on his oilskin and shot me a warm yet pain-racked smile. I knew exactly what he was thinking.

We stopped under a huge oak tree with gnarled roots and wide branches. The raindrops plopped off the outer leaves in a steady, almost comforting drone.

The bypass would cut straight through the heart of these trees.

"You read about things like this in the paper but you never think it's going to happen to you." Ash squatted down on his heels, his back pressed against the rough bark.

"I used to play under these trees as a kid." He pointed to a beech tree fanning out on the drive. "My dad used to tell me this was my heritage."

"Oh don't, Ash, please." I slid down beside him, taking in the gold blonde hair falling on his collar, the sea-blue eyes framed with thick black lashes, the flood of emotion all too obvious. Daisy bulldozed into me, slicking my cheeks with wet sloppy kisses.

"This time tomorrow they'll all be at the Town Hall sealing our fate. It looks like Stanley Preston got the last laugh after all."

"I hate him," I said with heartfelt passion, folding my fingers into Daisy's velvet soft coat.

"Oh Alex." Ash grabbed my hand and squeezed it with desperation. "What are we going to do?"

Back at the yard Zoe was filling in a magazine questionaire: *Just how seductive are you?*

"Would you wear perfume during the day, and if so would you carry it in your handbag?" Zoe pursed her lips with indecision. She then proceeded to tell me that if you rub olive oil into your eyelashes it makes them grow.

“Uh, no thank you. I think I’ll just remain short and stubby.”

I made a cup of coffee and gaped in amusement at Camilla in the arena riding Lace without any reins or stirrups. Eric was shouting instructions but sounded exasperated.

“What’s going on there?” It was the first time I’d ever seen Camilla on anyone but The Hawk.

Lace plodded round one-paced looking utterly bored and hardly lifting her legs two inches off the ground. Eric had Cam swinging her arms round in circles doing aerobics on horseback.

“Eric says Camilla is cardboard stiff and she either does some exercises or takes extra cod-liver oil to loosen her joints.”

“He’s really got her under his thumb.” I was amazed. “Or rather the hoof.”

“Yes, but the worm will turn,” Zoe warned. “Trust me, Cam’s about to blow a gasket.”

I could see exactly what Zoe meant.

Cam was turning blue in the face and looking worn to a frazzle. She was trying desperately to hitch her lower leg up the saddle flap following Eric’s orders, but was frantically losing her balance. Lace decided that was the perfect moment to dig in her heels and duck her head. Poor Cam went sailing off sideways, landing in a heap, legs sprawling everywhere, her hat lopsided and her mouth full of sand. Eric started to laugh.

"That's it." Cam staggered to her feet, apoplectic with rage, her mouth trembling. "I'm cold," she said. "I'm wet, I'm fed up, I'm sick to death of being bossed about." Her usually pale complexion flushed pink and white in quick succession. She threw down her whip which bounced off her boot and landed by Eric's wheelchair.

"Find yourself another team member to bully," she shrieked, eyes burning. "From this moment I quit!"

We were all dumbfounded. Eric's face flashed with pain and confusion and then the shutters came down and he was totally expressionless. Camilla stomped off to The Hawk's stable and slammed the door.

"She doesn't mean it," I said doubtfully. "She's just letting off steam."

Eric went home and another hour ticked by. Camilla was indulging in a major sulk.

"She's really hurt him, you know," I whispered, meaning Eric. "I know he's gruff and has all the diplomacy of a wild boar, but he really thought he was helping her. He does care."

"Maybe it's Cam you should be saying this to." Zoe pretended not to be worried. "If she spends any more time in that stable she'll turn into a horse."

I looked over the stable door bracing myself for a stream of abuse. Camilla was sitting on an upturned feed bucket, pouting ferociously.

I didn't know what to say.

"If you've come to try and change my mind, you're wasting your time." She glared at me with steely eyes. "He deserves all he gets."

I stood confused, stroking The Hawk's bony nose, trying to work out the best line of attack. Camilla pouted like an old-timer.

"We need you, Cam. Without you there's no team." I was prepared to grovel if I had to.

"Tough."

"You can't throw in the towel now, not after all our hard work."

She didn't answer.

"It wouldn't be fair to me and Zoe. Or Eric."

"Don't mention that slavedriver to me."

"Please, Cam, you can't do this to us." Panic fluttered in the pit of my stomach. It would be impossible to find another team member by Saturday.

"Do you honestly think the Trailblazers mean anything to me? I was just humouring you, trying to be nice for once. Now I wish I hadn't bothered."

"I don't believe you," I screeched, The Hawk pulling back looking unsure, my own self-control going up in smoke. "Why do you have to be so pig-headed? Stop being so self-centred for once and think about the team."

Camilla gaped and then glared. I was so angry I couldn't hold anything back. "You're not such a hotshot rider, you know. The Hawk carries you round . . . If you can't do it for me and Zoe, then at least do it for Eric – you owe him!"

I suddenly realized I'd gone too far.

Camilla was fuming. "I-I wouldn't go back on your team if you paid me," she sneered. "I don't care, do you hear me? It's all over. The Trailblazers are finished."

She stood up, head held high in victory. "Just see how you all manage without me!"

CHAPTER TEN

"I can't believe she's pulled out." I stomped out of Barney's stable.

I always knew Camilla was trouble – a leopard never changes its spots. It was obvious she'd ruin everything.

I thumped on my riding hat and led Barney out onto the gravel. It was the day of the committee meeting and the yard was like a morgue. Zoe had gone shopping, Eric wouldn't answer the phone and Ash was in the house burying himself in show schedules.

I was just swinging into the saddle when I saw the car. It didn't dawn on me who it was for at least thirty seconds. Then I saw the number plate – CC 100.

Mark Preston jumped out gaunt and strained. "Alex, I just want to talk."

I was panic-stricken. I urged Barney forward before I'd even found my stirrups.

"Alex . . ."

"Just get away from me, leave me alone." Barney broke into a trot, his ears twitching back and forth.

I thought that was the end of it, but Mark

wouldn't be put off. Next thing I knew he was catching us up in the car, cruising along, shouting through the window.

Barney tensed like a spring.

"Mark, stop it. You're scaring me."

"But you're not listening."

"Mark!"

All my anxiety was transmitting to Barney, who felt about to erupt. The car pressed closer, just feet away . . .

For a few seconds Barney dug in his heels, paralysed with terror, and then he threw up his head and from that moment everything seemed in fast-forward.

"Barney!" He hurled himself away, scrabbling for balance, clattering uncontrollably down the road.

"No!" The familiar sickening dread grabbed at my stomach and tied it in knots. It was ages since Barney had bolted. And the feeling of being totally out of control made my body turn to jelly.

We veered off into the parkland, thundering along, turf spraying up, the wood getting closer and closer.

I crouched forward, clutching with my knees, just trying to stay on. "Steady, boy. Steady."

He leapt over an open ditch as if it wasn't even there. Then we were in the wood. We were going too fast. He'd never keep his balance.

"Barney!"

The branch came at me from nowhere. I put out

an arm to save myself but it threw me back, the full force hitting my chest, yanking me from the saddle.

It suddenly dawned on me that I was about to fall off for the third time in as many weeks and it was really unfair.

As I smashed to the ground, it seemed to rise up to meet me, and stupidly I stuck out my hand and felt a juddering pain shoot right up my arm.

"Alex, wake up!"

I could just make out Ash staring down at me but everything else was a hazy blur.

"What's happened?" I struggled to get up and leant back quickly as my head threatened to blow off. My wrist was hurting like mad and I was covered in soil and strands of ivy.

"You were knocked out." Ash quickly pulled out a handkerchief and started dabbing at some blood on my upper lip. His hands were shaking. "God, Alex, you could have been killed!"

He quickly told me how Barney had gone back to the house, barging into the conservatory like a madman. Realising something was wrong, Ash had jumped on him and he'd led him here.

"Are you all right? Do you think you can stand up?"

We were at the bottom of a really steep bank in the old part of the wood that had been left to run wild. I didn't even remember falling down.

It was obvious what had knocked me out. I was leaning against a broken wall or something, all moss-covered and hidden. Ash bashed down a few nettles so I could stand up.

Suddenly his face changed colour – we stared at each other in amazement.

"It can't be, it just can't be." I scraped frantically at the carpet of moss with my good hand. Ash fell to his knees, ripping back ivy, hardly daring to believe it.

"It's got to be," I shrieked, grabbing hold of his shirt sleeve. "Look, it's some kind of well or something." I yanked off more ivy almost in a dream.

"We've got to find the Professor." Ash turned to me, his eyes brimming with emotion. "Alex, I think your accident might have saved the stables!"

"Third time lucky!" I winced.

The bank was steep, slippery and the only way out. Ash put my good arm round his shoulder and swung me into his arms. "Now for once in your life do as you're told and keep still."

Barney was tied to a branch at the top and went hysterical when he saw me. Ash levered me onto the front of the saddle and vaulted up behind. There wasn't a moment to lose.

We found the Professor outside Eric's cottage viewing the desolation which was once a lawn. Barney thundered up, coated in dried sweat, nostrils flared and pink.

"JD, quick, we need your help! You were right, we've found something!"

JD grabbed his Harley and we set off back into the woods. Barney was exhausted but kept on going. Ash took the Professor down the bank while I stood and waited, crossing my fingers and toes, praying to Barney that the ruins were Roman.

"I've got to get to the Town Hall!" JD appeared quicker than I expected, flushed and excited. "It's a brilliant find. Brilliant. And to think if you hadn't had that fall we'd never have found it."

"The meeting's already started." Ash looked at his watch, panic rising.

Barney neighed and solemnly pawed at the ground. "Not on you, you nitwit." JD eyed him with exasperation. "On the Harley!"

"I'm coming with you." Never had I been more determined. Ash gave me a look which meant "don't you dare" but I gritted my teeth and reached for the crash helmet.

"I'm not letting you go." Ash looked thunderous. "You should be seeing a doctor."

JD clambered onto the front. "Good God, girl. You've got more bottle than the Express Dairy."

The Harley roared like a fighter plane as I leapt on behind. We had to get to the Town Hall in time. We had to.

We burst through the main doors not even

checking at reception. "Excuse me, I really don't think you've got the authority . . ."

"Oh believe me, dear lady, I have." JD ran into a lift, dragging me with him. Sweat broke out on my forehead as undiluted pain torpedoed up my arm. The lift felt as if it was scaling Mount Everest.

"We've still got time!"

All I could think about were the stables and the bulldozers. And it all being flattened.

We practically fell through the boardroom door. Mr and Mrs Burgess were sitting at the far end, strained and tense. All I could see was a blur of grey faces and pinstripe suits.

"Gentlemen, there's been a development . . ."

Suddenly the blank faces started spinning round and round and my knees crumpled and I felt myself sliding.

"Goodness! The girl's fainted!"

"Well, don't keep me in the dark. I want to know everything!" Zoe was annoyed that she'd missed out on all the action.

I'd spent two hours in hospital having a fractured wrist set in plaster and would have rung her only my last twenty-pence coin went on a cup of coffee.

The bypass was temporarily postponed. The chances were they'd go back to route A which would be miles from the stable yard. It was brilliant. Just too good for words.

Barney was being treated like a hero and loving every minute. As soon as he saw me he plunged his big soft rubbery nose right in my face. "It's all right, Barney, I'm still alive," I told him as he slurped a huge kiss on my forehead. "I think he's been watching too many episodes of Casualty," I grinned. "He sees himself as a paramedic."

"After what he's done he can have anything he wants." Ash showered his neck with pats. "Portable television, cashmere rugs, gold-plated head collars – what do you say, old boy?" Barney snorted and pulled one of his old-fashioned looks as if Ash was stupid.

Eric arrived with Daisy who thundered up taking a flying leap and nearly knocking me sideways. But it was Barney she was really interested in.

Eric looked more emotional than I'd ever seen him. We didn't need words to describe the relief; there was a warmth and a camaraderie between us that spoke volumes. Against all the odds we'd fought back and won the day. We'd beaten the system.

The only cloud was seeing Camilla being dropped off by her mother and disappearing into The Hawk's stable. Luckily the phone rang at exactly the same moment so I was saved any embarrassment.

Mrs Brayfield's booming voice came on the line.

"Yes. Um. No, the Trailblazers won't be competing," I said, then listened to her news . . . "I see. Well, thanks for telling us."

I zapped the off button on the portable phone

and pushed the aerial back in with such ferocity it nearly broke off.

"The cheek of the man!"

Eric frowned and Ash looked genuinely alarmed. "What on earth's the matter?"

I told them that apparently Stanley Preston had invested in three superb Connemara ponies brought over specially from Ireland and loaned them to one of the Pony Club teams.

The Bevan brothers were three obnoxious boys, all red-headed, with the energy of setters. Crispin, Justin and Damien. Zoe had never forgiven them for nicknaming her "Golf Club" because her figure went straight up and down and she wore huge clumpy shoes at school.

Connemaras are known for being fabulous jumping ponies and in Ireland they pop over Normandy banks as part of their general routine. Stanley Preston was being spiteful and childish and using his money to get back at us.

"They're calling themselves the Gladiators," I said, and Zoe cracked out laughing. In PE Justin and Crispin couldn't even manage a dumbell.

Eric looked about to burst. "I can't bear to be made a fool of." He was almost gnashing his teeth.

It was perfectly within the rules to borrow ponies. Stanley Preston had got the last laugh.

None of us saw Camilla approaching, not until

she was on top of us. Her blonde hair was pulled back in a stiff bow and her eyes were puffy and swollen.

"I – I think I might have overreacted." She fumbled with her hands and then met Eric's eyes. "I wondered if you might consider having me back?"

It was probably the first time Camilla had admitted she was wrong in her life. It took guts, I had to give her that.

"Gladly." Eric warmed to her. "But that still only makes two team members, as the other one is up to her elbow in plaster."

"I'm riding," I said in a steel-edged voice.

Eric stared at me contemplatively, weighing up the pros and cons, drumming his fingers on his lips. "Well, in that case you'd better get Mrs Brayfield back on the phone. Tell her the Trailblazers are back in. And come hell or high water, they're going to win!"

CHAPTER ELEVEN

"Where's my lucky whip?" I raced out of the common room with my white shirt buttoned up wrong and my hair fighting its way out of a hairnet.

Judy was expertly plaiting Barney who for once stood like an angel. Camilla arrived with jeans over her clean jods and armed with tail gloss, hair spray and white chalk.

Zoe had been polishing Lace for hours and she looked absolutely fantastic. Her cream tail was done up in a French plait and Zoe was just about to apply quarter markings, a stencilled pattern on her rump.

"Watch the hoof oil!" she shrieked as I upended the grooming box looking for a black whip with a red thong.

Ash came out of the house pulling on a rugby shirt. "Where's Eric? He said he'd be here at 8.30."

"Is that the time?" I'd wasted an hour at home trying to find a short-sleeved shirt and my painkillers, which Mum had moved.

Ash started reading the dressage test out to Camilla.

"I'm terrified," she said, turning white.

"Don't panic," I flapped. "Just don't panic."

Ash turned the horsebox round at nine and by nine thirty we had the horses loaded. Eric arrived carrying three stopwatches and the Trailblazers shirts. "Right, I think we're ready."

The showground was a sea of mud and people skidding around in wellies. Ash expertly manoeuvred the lorry through a gateway and past the Bevans' box which had got stuck. Crispin was being dragged around by a dun with a Roman nose and looked quite ill.

The competition was already under way with the tannoy blaring and Mrs Brayfield strutting around in a tweed jacket with a plastic daffodil in the lapel.

A competitor galloped across the cross-country finish line dripping in water and shaking his head in grim despair. "It's hopeless," I heard him complaining to one of the stewards. His pony looked about to drop. "That water should be roped off, it's dangerous."

Camilla went off to collect our numbers while I struggled with my black show jacket which wouldn't go over my plaster. Eric snapped at Ash for forgetting the binoculars and at Zoe for a speck of dirt on her saddle. The tension was unbearable.

Camilla trudged back with the news that nobody had yet gone clear cross-country and the Normandy bank was proving unjumpable.

"Poppycock." Eric bashed the arm of his wheelchair. "Ash, get round that course and find out what's going on. Zoe, Camilla, get these horses tacked up. I want all three of you in the warm-up ring pronto. Alex – behind the horsebox – now."

I obeyed. "What is it? What's the matter?"

"Listen." His voice was serious. "Camilla's losing her bottle; Zoe's never had what it takes. I'm relying on you to get round clear. Are you sure you're OK?"

"Yes."

"OK then. Use your right hand as much as possible. Save all your energy until the last few fences – that's when the trouble starts. Try to use the strength in your shoulder. And for goodness' sake hang on."

Eric had spent the previous evening showing me videos of Ginny Elliot and how she managed to hold strong horses even with an arm weakened from a horrific twenty-three breaks.

"You can do it, I know you can. Just keep believing it."

Cam went into the dressage jittery but remembering to hold her head high. The Hawk was trying his very best.

"Come on, Cam, just keep your concentration."

The judges were sitting in a caravan at the far end jotting down notes. Two kids got told off by a steward for swinging on a rope.

"Yes!" Eric clenched his fist as The Hawk came out after performing the best test of his life. "That's my girl!"

Zoe moved up next, anxiety etched all over her face. Out of the three horses Lace was by far the best at dressage. This was where we needed a good mark.

"Go on, Zoe. Strut your stuff."

Lace trotted into the arena balanced and elegant and did a perfect halt.

"Steady, girl, steady. Take your time." Eric was on tenterhooks.

Suddenly I noticed Stanley Preston march across to the opposite end with Mark on one side and Damien Bevan on the other, mounted on a snowy grey 14.2 which looked as if it had rockets under its hoofs.

"What the—" I started.

He had a word with one of the judges and then stood, arms crossed, watching Zoe.

"The pig," I flamed. "He's trying to put her off. He's staring her out."

Zoe didn't seem to notice. But then instead of going across the arena she went down the long side and immediately the bell pealed to say she'd taken the wrong course. Flustered and red-faced she picked up where she'd gone wrong but it wiped out any chance of a good mark.

Preston deliberately walked past us so he was in earshot. "Pathetic," he smirked. "God knows what the yellow nag will do. Can you believe the old man thinks he's a champion?"

Damien let out a false laugh and desperately tried to hang on to the plunging grey.

Zoe came out of the arena with tears glistening in her eyes. "I'm so sorry," she started, "I've let everybody down."

"You've let nobody down," Eric snapped. "You did your best and that's what counts."

We had an hour before Barney was due to do his test and the showjumping began. We walked the cross-country course and scared ourselves to death, although Ash gave us a professional rundown on how to jump each fence.

The whole showground was chaotic with riders, parents, spectators all milling round, all trying to be everywhere at once. Mrs Brayfield was at her wits' end trying to keep the showjumping to time. One girl from the Pink Panther team had locked herself in her horsebox and refused to come out. The First Aid tent was packed and the burger stall had somehow caught fire and had to be evacuated.

The Sutton Vale in-crowd were all strutting round in dark sunglasses and tight jodhpurs trying to look ultra-glamorous. Zoe was agog when we caught a glimpse of Jasper Carrington in the saddlery tent looking at a martingale. He had buckets of money and usually a different girlfriend every week. A willowy blonde with a chocolate-brown tan trotted after him laden down with rugs and bandages and a trailing bridle.

"Damien Bevan clear at the water, going like a steam train." The commentary crackled into life, bristling with excitement. "Just look at this pony go, what a star."

A flash of white glinted through the trees and then the red and black colours of the Gladiators came into view, storming up the hill to the finish line.

"How are we going to beat that?" Zoe was utterly defeated.

Damien yanked the Connemara pony to a halt, stood up in the saddle and leapt off like one of the famous jockeys.

It was the first clear round of the day.

Stanley Preston was gloating like the cat who'd got the cream.

"Blast!" I turned on my heel and marched back to the horsebox, determination bubbling up inside me. When the going gets tough, the tough get going. I had something to prove.

Eric and Ash were nowhere to be found but Camilla was standing by the groom's door puffing away on a cigarette.

"What on earth do you think you're doing?" I snatched it out of her mouth and stamped it into the wet ground. "You stupid idiot, that's not going to solve anything."

Her mouth dropped open in shock. "Well we haven't all got your guts, have we?" Her hands were literally shaking. "It's Eric, he expects so much. I can't do it."

"There's no such word as 'can't'." Eric came up

behind us, taking in the scene at one glance. Zoe was with him.

"So that's it, is it? We let Stanley Preston walk all over us. Give up at the first hurdle?"

"No, no . . ." Zoe looked doubtful.

"We can win this competition. I know we can. But you've got to believe it yourselves. In your hearts. And as for you, Camilla." Eric's face softened with encouragement. "You've got the ability: you can either excel, or be mediocre. The choice is yours."

"I'd better get the tack." Zoe disappeared into the horsebox.

We needed three showjumping clears and a good dressage test from Barney.

The sweat was pouring down my back as I entered the ring. Barney seemed to grow two inches as a wave of applause broke out from the crowd. Everybody knew about my broken wrist. I tightened my hands on the reins and Barney tensed and waited for my next instructions. "Ride like a champion, look like a champion, be a champion." Eric's words filled my head. "And most of all believe in yourself."

We moved off into a perfect canter . . .

When we'd finished I heard Zoe going bananas. "That was brilliant!" Camilla was clapping like mad, Eric was as proud as punch. Barney put in a cheeky buck as we left the ring, which had everybody laughing.

"I didn't know you could ride like that." Cam was awestruck. "You do realize . . ." she was clutching my bad arm in excitement, "we've shot straight into the lead!"

Ash and Judy came over with Lace and The Hawk, tightening girths and adjusting nosebands for the showjumping. Judy had a lead rope round her neck, a mane comb in her mouth and a set of rubber reins over her arm. Daisy was tripping her up at the same time. "Cam, you're in the jumping now – the steward's called your name three times."

The Hawk quickly pinged over a practice fence and charged into the showjumping arena with his tail bandage still in place.

"Remember, steady," Eric bawled after her. "She's going too fast," he grumbled as The Hawk scuffed up a cloud of turf and shied nervously at the double planks. "She's forgotten everything."

But all the training paid off.

"A clear round!" the commentator announced. And ten minutes later: "A clear round for Zoe Jackson."

As for Barney, he rattled the last pole. Everybody gasped as it rolled back and forth and then lazily plopped to the ground. Four faults. We were still hanging on to the lead, but only by the skin of our teeth.

"You'll lose." Stanley Preston pushed through

the crowds, his eyes narrowed with anger. "We'll cream you, just you wait and see."

I thought he was going to grab hold of Barney's rein but at the same moment my parents appeared, together with Zoe's mum Patsy, and the Professor and Jenny, which diffused the situation.

"What did *he* want?" Zoe looked worried.

"We've got him rattled," I grinned. "He knows we're in with a fighting chance."

"I'm glad he thinks so," Zoe mumbled. "Camilla's disappeared to the loo for the fifth time."

The cross-country was the all-important phase. We had to do well. Three clears and no less.

Zoe munched through two hamburgers with double onions which she said steadied her nerves, and I swallowed a painkiller with a swig of coke. Camilla sat in the horsebox with her head between her knees.

"Hold her up at the bank." Eric hammered out instructions. "Kick on for the water and steady for the last."

Zoe made her way down to the start with Lace looking fit but calm. A heavy cob plunged off in front and then it was Zoe's turn.

"Good luck," I shouted.

And then the countdown. "Three. Two. One. Go!"

"She's over the palisade!" Eric had the Professor's binoculars trained on the wood. "She's clear at the coffin. Come on, girl, come on!"

Camilla moved off to the start with Ash and Judy as a back-up team. I stayed to watch Zoe, rooting for her with every fibre of my body. Lace was a cream speck flitting through the trees.

"She's over the bank!" Eric was going hoarse. "She's nearly home!"

"Number 29 fallen at the water." The commentator's voice was deadpan. Number 29 was Zoe. We couldn't see a thing!

"She's remounted and carrying on – brave girl."

Where *was* she? The disappointment was terrible. A fall was sixty penalties. We'd lost all chance.

Zoe cantered over the finish line minutes later looking absolutely drenched and shattered. Lace had mud plastered all up her right side.

"I'm so sorry." She slithered from the saddle, her jodhpurs sodden. "It all happened so fast."

Tears suddenly sprung into her eyes and she bolted for the horsebox, leaving Lace with Eric.

"Zoe!" I charged after her trying not to draw too much attention, which was impossible. "Zoe!"

"I'm OK, all right? Just leave me alone, I'll be fine."

"It was just bad luck," I said. "It could have happened to anybody. You were riding like a pro."

"No I wasn't." She changed into a dry shirt and blew her nose on a tissue. "I wasn't pushing hard enough – I've let everybody down. You wouldn't have fallen off."

"That's rubbish, and you know it."

"Do I?"

"Yes. And anyway, we're a team, aren't we? We stick together, we pull each other through. And right now, Cam's out there on the course and she needs our support. We can't let her down."

"Well, you'll just have to manage without me."

"Oh no, Miss Jackson." I picked up her discarded riding hat and thrust it at her. "You're made of tougher stuff than that. If you give up now then it's all over. I'll refuse to ride."

"There you are!" Judy was anxiously leading Lace round with a sweat sheet slung over her quarters.

Eric looked so relieved to see Zoe. He took in her flushed face. "You got round, girl. That's the most important thing."

"Have you heard?" Judy said, frantically feeding Lace mints, her eyes shining. "Damien Bevan fell off at the first fence. We're still in with a chance."

"Camilla Davies clear at the log pile, still going strong."

Camilla was out on the course and going like the clappers.

"Look at her go!" Eric grabbed the binoculars from Ash. The Hawk scorched through the wood and leapt the palisade two strides out.

"Hang on, Cam!" The coffin loomed up next.

"The girl's inspired." Eric was rigid with excitement. At this rate she could get the best time of the day. It could put us back in contention.

"Legs, legs, legs," Eric shouted, though Cam couldn't hear. The Hawk corkscrewed over the last and blasted up to the finish.

"She's done it!" Zoe was jumping up and down.

Cam slid off, purple in the face and out of breath. "Watch the water," she gasped. "It's like a skating rink."

Just at that moment Judy led Barney across, tacked up and with his head held high like an old professional, his flanks quivering with excitement. It was all down to us, we were the last ride of the day.

The next half an hour was frantic. Ash had to cut a sleeve out of my cross-country shirt and help me on with the back protector.

Judy slapped grease on Barney's forearms to help him slip over the fences if he happened to hit one. It was important not to apply it so high that it could touch the reins and make them slippery. Then she looped a bootlace round the bridle headpiece and tied it to the first plait to prevent the bridle coming off if we fell.

If we fell. Nerves churned in my stomach like a cement mixer. Judy tightened the girth by two holes and rammed down the stirrups. I put on my jockey skull and adjusted the chin strap. It was now or never.

Zoe clipped on the lead rope and we moved down to the start.

"Now remember," Eric said, walking next to me, "try to keep to a rhythm – no stopping and starting. And if he does get too strong, pull up. It's not worth risking life and limb."

I settled down into the saddle and tried to stay calm. Sharron Davies, the Olympic swimmer, had once competed with two broken wrists; I was determined to do it with one.

"Stand by." The starter looked harassed and exhausted. I circled at walk and tried to focus.

Suddenly Mark Preston ducked under the rope and rushed over, making straight for Barney.

"I'm sorry." His face crumpled with guilt. "That's what I wanted to say at the stables. I never meant any harm." He reached up to stroke Barney's neck but I reined him away.

"Alexandra Johnson, thirty seconds."

Barney half reared in excitement, knowing the procedure. "Hold steady."

"Good luck." Zoe was standing by the ropes with Cam. "Three, two, one – *go*!"

Barney bounded forward. I shifted both reins into my right hand and angled for the first fence. "Steady, boy. Not too fast." He immediately settled back, almost as if he knew I needed looking after.

We took the first four fences in our stride.

"Good boy. Come on, you can do it." I patted

his neck and he moved forward with an extra spurt of speed.

Uphill for the palisade, over the hanging log. He was jumping like a champion, eating up the ground. Foot perfect.

All I had to do was hang on.

The Normandy bank loomed up, a solid mass. Barney checked, pricked up his ears, cat-leapt on to the top and sprung off on all fours. He was doing it himself, working it all out.

"Come on, boy, come on." There was a long gallop between the bank and the water. I crouched low over his back, urging him on. The steward blew the whistle and spectators quickly cleared a path. Water is one of the most difficult obstacles. It takes complete trust between horse and rider. We had to get it just right.

I hardly remember the take-off. A sudden wave of nausea swept over me and I slumped in the saddle. The steward ran forward. Barney pounded on, his eyes fixed on the jump ahead. Nobody had taken the direct route all day. Barney was heading straight for the highest part of the jump. The water on the other side would be up to his shoulder.

A huge groan rose from the crowd.

Barney bunched his muscles and prepared to launch. We half lifted up and then his back legs skidded underneath him. He cracked the top part of the fence, skewed to one side, found another leg and slithered over.

We plunged into the water full force. His knees buckled and his head submerged. "Barney!"

Water sprayed into my face, into my eyes, my mouth.

"He's found his feet!" someone shouted from the ropes.

Barney heaved up, throwing me back into the saddle, and thundered forward.

We scraped over the log out and a huge roar went up from the crowds.

"What a horse!" A man ran forward to help as Barney stopped to shake himself but I screamed at him to stay away. Any outside help would get us disqualified.

Soaked, exhausted, trembling, Barney surged forward towards the finish. I clung to the saddle, gritting my teeth. Barney was fighting for every stride, determined to get home. We could do it, I knew we could.

I saw Cam and Ash in the distance, their faces strained, their fists clenched, urging us on. Mark Preston bobbed forward on my right. A few more strides. Just one more effort.

Suddenly we were surrounded by people. We could have been Grand National winners. Someone grabbed Barney's reins and undid his noseband. I saw Mum and Dad looking completely overwhelmed.

Then Ash's arms were round me, lifting me out of the saddle. I was still clinging to a handful of mane.

Eric was right there in his wheelchair, and just seeing his face made me brim up with tears. I gave him a hug and he made a joke about me covering him in water. Then he squeezed my hand and we didn't need words. We weren't going to stop here. We were going right to the top.

Barney paraded round like a champion and Cam and Zoe raced back to the horsebox to fetch Lace and The Hawk.

We had won the team trophy. Barney had come first individually but it was the team that really mattered. We'd all pulled together when it counted most. Eric couldn't have asked for more.

I caught a brief glimpse of Preston's gold Rolls-Royce roaring out of the car park and I couldn't resist a smile.

Then I threw my arms round Barney's neck and patted him as if it was going out of fashion. We'd proved we weren't a flash in the pan, a one-event wonder. Barney had talent, he was a horse in a million. As for me, I felt like an Olympic champion!

GLOSSARY

anti-cast roller A stable **roller** which prevents the horse from becoming **cast** in the stable or box.

Badminton One of the world's greatest three-day events, staged each year at Badminton House, Gloucestershire.

to **bank** When a horse lands on the middle part of an obstacle (e.g. a **table**), it is said to have banked it.

bit The part of the bridle which fits in the mouth of the horse, and to which the reins are attached.

bounce A type of jump consisting of two fences spaced so that as the horse lands from the first, it takes off for the next, with no strides in between.

bridle The leather **tack** attached to the horse's head which helps the rider to control the horse.

cast When a horse is lying down against a wall in a stable or box and is unable to get up, it is said to be cast.

chef d'équipe The person who manages and sometimes captains a team at events.

colic A sickness of the digestive system. Very dangerous for horses because they cannot be sick.

collected canter A slow pace with good energy.

crop A whip.

cross-country A gallop over rough ground, jumping solid natural fences. One of the three eventing disciplines. (The others are **dressage** and **showjumping.**)

dressage A discipline in which rider and horse perform a series of movements to show how balanced, controlled, etc. they are.

dun Horse colour, generally yellow dun. (Also blue dun.)

feed room Store room for horse food.

forearm The part of the foreleg between elbow and knee.

girth The band which goes under the stomach of a horse to hold the **saddle** in place.

Grackle A type of noseband which stops the horse opening its mouth wide or crossing its jaw. Barney is wearing one on the cover of *Will to Win*.

hand A hand is 10 cm (4 in) – approximately the width of a man's hand. A horse's height is given in hands.

hard mouth A horse is said to have a hard mouth if it does not respond to the rider's commands through the **reins** and **bit**. It is caused by over-use of the reins and bit: the horse has got used to the pressure and thus ignores it.

head collar A headpiece without a **bit**, used for leading and tying-up.

horsebox A vehicle designed specifically for the transport of horses.

horse trailer A trailer holding one to three horses, designed to be towed by a separate vehicle.

jockey skull A type of riding hat, covered in brightly coloured silks or nylon.

jodhpurs Type of trousers/leggings worn when riding.

lead rope Used for leading a horse. (Also known as a "shank".)

livery Stables where horses are kept at the owners' expense.

loose box A stable or area, where horses can be kept.

manege Enclosure for schooling a horse.

manger Container holding food, often fixed to a stable wall.

martingale Used to regulate a horse's head carriage.

numnah Fabric pad shaped like a saddle and worn underneath one.

one-day event Equestrian competition completed over one day, featuring **dressage, showjumping** and **cross-country.**

one-paced Describes a horse which prefers to move at a certain pace, and is unwilling to speed up or increase its stride.

palisade Type of cross-country jump.

Palomino A horse with a gold-coloured body and white mane or tail.

Pelham bit A bit with a curb chain and two **reins,** for use on horses that are hard to stop.

Pony Club International youth organization, founded to encourage young people to ride.

reins Straps used by the rider to make contact with a horse's mouth and control it.

roller Leather or webbing used to keep a rug or blanket in place. Like a belt or girth which goes over the withers and under the stomach.

saddle Item of tack which the rider sits on. Gives security and comfort and assists in controlling the horse.

showjumping A course of coloured jumps that can be knocked down. Shows how careful and controlled horse and rider are.

snaffle bit The simplest type of **bit.**

spread Type of jump involving two uprights at increasing heights.

square halt Position where the horse stands still with each leg level, forming a rectangle.

steeplechasing A horse race with a set number of obstacles including a water jump. Originally a cross-country race from steeple to steeple.

stirrups Shaped metal pieces which hang from the saddle by leather straps and into which riders place their feet.

surcingle A belt or strap used to keep a day or night rug in position. Similar to a **roller,** but without padding.

table A type of jump built literally like a table, with a flat top surface.

tack Horse-related items.

tack room Where **tack** is stored.

take-off The point when a horse lifts its forelegs and springs up to jump.

three-day event A combined training competition, held over three consecutive days. Includes **dressage, cross-country** and **showjumping.** Sometimes includes roads and tracks.

tiger trap A solid fence meeting in a point with a large ditch underneath. Large ones are called elephant traps.

upright A normal single showjumping fence.

Weymouth bit Like a **Pelham bit,** but more severe.

Samantha Alexander

RIDERS 3

Peak Performance

"He's here!" Zoe burst through the tack room door, a head collar and lead rope trailing after her. "It's Joel, he's here. He's at the house!"

My boyfriend, Ash, came in after her. "He's only a trainer, for goodness' sake. Anybody would think he's the Prime Minister."

Joel O'Ryan, champion three-day eventer, has come to run a course at the local pony club. He's famous for turning young riders into stars. Alex is desperate to catch his eye but in doing so she risks losing both Ash and her trainer, Eric . . .